Holy Matrimony

God Created the Family

Before He Created the Church

Library of Congress Cataloging-in-Publication Data

Book Cover Design by, Angela Boone

Scriptures taken from King James & Amplified Bible, Old and New Testament copyright © 1965, 1987 by the Zondervan Corporation. The Amplified New & Old Testament copyright 1958, 1987 by The Lockman Foundation, and The NIV Copyright 1973, 1978, 1984, by International Bible Society. Used by permission of Zondervan. Scriptures taken from The Message, Copyright 1993, 1994, 1995, 1996, 2000, 2001, 2002. Used by permission of NavPress Publishing Group".

This book is dedicated to all of the women
who are suffering in silent.
You are not alone and the devil is a liar.
"No weapon that is formed against you shall prosper".
God will deliver you out of any bad situation.
Step into your purpose today and choose to be victorious.
Stop compromising your salvation.

This Is A Gift For:

_____

Name

_____

From

_____

Date

This book belongs to you and your account is credited.
The Bible says, "My people are destroyed for the lack of knowledge.
Keep this book in your private library so you will not be destroyed for
the lack of knowledge.

FOREWORD

God is a covenant God and He stands sure behind everything He institutes. Holy Matrimony offers insight into the mental abuses that are prevalent in marital relationships today. It exposes the deceit and damage that is done as a result of sin, perversion and wickedness. Behind the closed doors of many homes across America and the world, there are circumstances that the enemy uses to divide and conquer covenant partners for his control. Even the enemy understands the power of unity. Ecclesiastes 4:12, states this, though one may be overpowered by another, two can withstand him. And a threefold cord is not quickly broken. This is definitely the key, if a Man and Woman are truly joined and they rely and acknowledge God and seek His will while not leaning to their own understanding, God will direct their marital path. To God marriage is honorable and only a wise Man and Woman understands this.

God has chosen Angela Boone for such a time as this, to proclaim infallible truths without compromise. This book will stir others who have been afraid to come forth to uncover ungodliness in all facets of their marriage and in the Body of Christ.

Ms. Boone used her experience to war against ungodliness, rather than to sit and be pitiful and miserable about her circumstances. Some have been driven to seek the world's way of handling hurt. Angela Boone chose to use the two edged sword of the spirit to effectively speak to the hearts of others who are secretly and without spiritual support living a lie. Certainly the enemy meant it for evil, but God is about to turn things around for His good, because a woman of God stepped into her divine calling.

This book was inspired by The Holy Ghost to a Woman ready to proclaim the uncontaminated word of God to those captive in wicked marital relationships. This book is highly rated and a must read!

Minister Phinell Franklin

5

Marriage is honorable in all, and the bed undefiled:
but whoremongers and adulterers God will judge.
Hebrews 13:4

CONTENTS

INTRODUCTION 8
HOW I MET MY HUSBAND-TO-BE 13
THE NIGHT BEFORE THE MARRIAGE 20
THE MARRIAGE VOWS 29
IN HINDSIGHT 36
HOW I WAS PUT OUT OF THE CHURCH (Part One) 40
THE STORY OF OUR SEPARATION 48
HOW I WAS PUT OUT OF THE CHURCH (Part Two) 67
MOVING ON—THE AFTERMATH 85
HOW GOD REVEALS OUR LIVES TO US 96
GOSSIP AND BACKBITERS IN GOD'S HOUSE 107
HOW IT ALL STARTED—THE BIBLICAL PERSPECTIVE 121
    Introduction 121
    In the Beginning 124
    A Help Meet for Adam 128
    The Mother of Sin 130
    The Transgression 132
    Good Seed, Bad Seed—Cain and Abel 137
    The Covenant and Covet Relationship 143
HUSBANDS, WIVES, AND MARRIAGE IN THE EYES OF GOD 149
    What is a Husband in the Eyes of God? 149
    What is a Wife in the Eyes of God? 154
    The Separation 162
    Christian Holy Matrimony 169
    Marriage 172
MEN WHO WOULD RUIN A WOMAN'S LIFE 176
    Low Down, Down Low 176
    Characteristics of Men Who Would Ruin Your Life 184
HOPE FOR A NEW DAY 193
    Christ is Coming 193
    Words of Encouragement 193
    Scriptures for Protection 195
    Prosperity 200
    Healing 206
    Change Your Life 212
    A Prayer for Strength through the Spirit 213
    A Fight to the Finish 216
NOTES 219

INTRODUCTION

Today, the institution of marriage is at the center of a great controversy; various groups are seeking to redefine it, from the men that consider themselves on the "down low"[1], to gays and lesbians seeking to marry, to others promoting group marriages. These efforts are undermining a union that has been critical to maintaining the foundation of society. HOLY MATRIMONY describes the importance of this union from a Christian perspective—a perspective that emphasizes that marriage should be considered a holy union between a man and a woman. It discusses how this union is being destroyed, and how, in the process, this destruction is not only undermining God's plan according to the Bible, but is jeopardizing the stability of society as a whole. For example, consider the high number of AIDS cases we see today, particularly amongst the African-

---

[1] This expression refers to men who are in heterosexual relationships, married or otherwise, but who are secretly sleeping around with other men (and possibly with other women as well).

American community. Surely, the reasons for this include 1) the increase in open and non-marital sexual relations and 2) the decrease in people's appreciation and valuation of marriage and monogamy (meaning one-on-one relationships).

This book draws upon my own experiences, where I was married to a bishop in an African-American gospel church—a bishop who turned out to be living a secret double life involving adultery and prostitution. In addition, it draws upon the Biblical teachings about what a marriage should be, ranging from the beginning of a relationship to problems that occur in the marriage to what to do about these problems.

Bowing to my readers' requests, I am going to share different encounters that happened in my marriage, but I will also draw upon the scriptures at the end of my story. These scriptures have carried me through the worst times in my life and in my marriage. In trying to restore my marriage, I received something more; while praying for my marriage, I received a healing in my own life.

As I prayed and cried for God to heal my marriage, what I didn't realize was that God was healing me. Through my prayers and by God's grace, when I was delivered out of that marriage, I never hated my husband, nor the women and men who mistreated me in his congregation. My marriage was under attack by demonic forces, but out of it all, I received from God a relationship that I never knew existed—an intimate relationship that took me to another level, while God protected my children and me.

After reading my previously published book, *Live What U Preach Preachers,* people said about my marriage experience that the signs were there and that I was crazy for going through with it. My brother-in-law saw what was happening, so why couldn't I? What was wrong with me? Why did I go through with that marriage in the first place?

We all have opinions about what someone else should or shouldn't have done. But none of us really knows what we will do until we are put in a similar situation. Love is blind, and we've all done things in our lives that some of us regret and some of us don't regret. I don't regret a moment of what happened to me in that marriage; it taught me so much. Now, though, the only way such a marriage would ever happen again, is if I hadn't learned anything from the first experience. Hopefully, we will each learn from our mistakes and move on.

I share my experiences and understanding with you, because I now believe that we go through these things in order to help someone else. Through our experiences, and by sharing them afterward, we become a blessing in another person's life. I remember hearing a well-known bishop say, "Don't take this the wrong way, but if you haven't went through nothing, I don't want you around me, because you can't feel my pain." In other words, if you haven't walked through the valleys, how can I show you the hills I have since climbed?

In this book, I will also discuss the importance of Holy Matrimony and how, from a Christian perspective, to save and preserve it.

Before going any further, I would like to share some of the events that took place before I met my husband.

HOW I MET MY HUSBAND-TO-BE

For years, I had known that I would be where God wanted me to be by the time I turned forty. As it came to pass, I was in a church on the other side of town, when, by my fortieth birthday, I was baptized and filled with the Holy Ghost (spirit).

The church was located in Warren, Michigan. I was there praising the Lord. I didn't know anything about the church of God and Christ or any of the organizations that some churches have. One day, while in prayer, with my eyes closed and arms lifted high up in the air, a man came over to me and said, "God wants to use you, but you have to have an ear to hear." After service, I didn't know who it was that was talking to me. Outside the church, though, my attention was drawn toward an older man and his wife getting into their truck to leave. The husband reminded me of the pictures we see of Jesus, with the long salt-and-pepper hair. My spirit drew me to these people, and I said to the man, "Was that you talking to me in church today?" He just smiled and hugged me. After they left, I never saw him or his wife again.

On another occasion, a friend—the one friend who I was very close to in church—told me that God was really 'growing me up quick in His word.' I never really paid any attention to these kind of experiences; I just continued on praising the Lord.

About two months later, I was getting out of bed one time when out of the blue, a voice spoke to me, as though someone was in the room with me. The voice said, "Everywhere you go, thousands of people will hear you speak." I started crying and praising the Lord and couldn't stop all day. I couldn't believe that I would be speaking in front of anyone; the thought of it was too terrifying.

But then I started writing. If you'd known me in school, you'd know that I wasn't a writer. But God! Through the Holy Ghost spirit of the Lord, I became a writer. As I wrote, I wanted to write like Paul in the Bible. We really have to be careful what we ask for.

After the spirit of God spoke to me that day, every night after that, I would feel the presence of the Lord from my head to my toes, comforting me. Prior to this, I couldn't sleep for a long time; I would wake up every night at the same time, and I'd worry about everything. Now I could sleep again. When that comfort came, my worries dissolved, and I've slept like a baby every night since.

I should also mention that I was the owner of my own construction company—one of a very few black females in my field. God was showing me favor, and I was very happy and content. But then came a day that would change my life for ever.

I met a man who was running for mayor, and because of the business I was in, he was planning to do some construction and wanted me to be a part of the project. After some months of meeting with him, he asked me if I knew of a certain Bishop Woody, whose picture was hanging on his wall. I told him that I'd never heard of the man. Everyone knows him, he said. Everyone but me, I replied. So, being good at setting up meetings for people to network and talk about business opportunities, this man called Bishop Woody and set up a meeting.

When I first met Bishop Woody, he seemed like a very nice person, and I'm always looking for good business opportunities for my company… that's my job. So, off to lunch we went. We had a great time talking, and the lunch was good. Then, when dessert came, Bishop Woody and I ended up sharing a dessert; I don't usually do that, but somehow, on this day, it just happened that way.

The day after the meeting, I started getting phone calls from him. I told my secretary to tell him that I wasn't in. I didn't know what he wanted, but I was also not interested. Why would I be? After all, God was taking such good care of me: his favor was upon my children and me, I had recently picked up an airport project, and I was working on a twenty-six million dollar contract in Florida. But Bishop Woody would not stop calling me. So, one day I thought, what the heck, he's left his number with my secretary, so I returned his call.

We started talking about his project, and, in the course of the conversation, he told me to be careful of the man who introduced us, because he was "scandalous." Although this seemed like a strange thing to say about the man who had just introduced us, I didn't give it much thought at the time. I thought Bishop Woody was nice, so we ended up talking on a regular basis. He was very nice to me in these first days. At the time, he was recording a new

CD, and I would go with him to the studio. We would see each other every day, often meeting for breakfast, lunch, and dinner.

After about three months, Bishop Woody asked me to marry him. I thought he was just joking. But then he arranged for me to meet his mother, which showed me how serious he really was. We all met for lunch. His mother didn't like me, though—I could tell. At the time, I didn't know why, but I found out later.

One day, we went to visit another church—we offered fellowship with other churches—and Bishop Woody asked me to ride with him, so I did. After service, apparently his mother asked, "Who's that in the car with Woody?" Some of the people from our church said, "It's Angel."

Well, Bishop Woody's mother called him the next day on his cell phone. We were in the studio at the time.

She said to him, "You're a bishop, and you need to act a certain way." I couldn't see that we had done anything wrong or out of the ordinary. It seemed as though she just didn't like me. It wasn't that simple, though. I found out later that there were things—dirty little secrets, so to speak—that she didn't want me or anybody else to know about.

So, with me being oblivious to the reasons behind Bishop Woody's mother's dislike of me, the relationship continued—all the way to the altar.

THE NIGHT BEFORE THE MARRIAGE

Looking out the window of the Detroit Omni Hotel on a typical October evening, excitement and mixed emotions consumed me. I hadn't heard from my fiancé all day. Tomorrow was the big day. Shouldn't he be concerned and interested in how his bride-to-be was handling the prospect of our new life together? Perhaps I was being too sensitive, I thought, so I turned my attention to the events ahead. Pulling myself away from my fixation on the downtown skyline, I decided to call my mother. As I reached for the phone, though, I couldn't help glancing at the clock next to it and noticing that it was already 10pm. So much for trying to turn my attention to other things. It was 10pm the night before my wedding and I hadn't heard from my husband-to-be all day. What was going on here? Surely, this wasn't normal.

In the turmoil of my mixed emotions, I relived in my mind the day I excitedly rushed to the church to show off our beautiful wedding invitations. Before I could open the box of invitations, though, Bishop Woody snatched them out of my hand, yelling at me that people could see his name through the envelope. I was very hurt and quite confused. It seemed as though he didn't want his name to be seen on the wedding invitations. Not only this, but he didn't tell his congregation about his wedding plans until two weeks before the wedding.

So, now I sat in that Detroit hotel, with the day just about over, and I hadn't heard a word from him. For all he knew, I could have broken out in hives, been running with diarrhea, or been throwing up from the stress. It was close to midnight when the phone rang. I remember the time, because I couldn't sleep. I was so churned up that I didn't remember most of the conversation, except him telling me that he was at a local department store. My first thought was that he was spending the money I had given him the day before. But then I remembered that he had used that money to buy some alligator shoes. For some reason, I was reminded of a time two months after we met when he had asked me to loan him seven thousand dollars for a project he was working on—a CD recording. Luckily, though, I didn't end up loaning it to him.

Shortly after hanging up the phone, I dozed off to sleep and had the strangest dream. I was rushing to the church, fully dressed in my wedding gown, arriving only to discover that the wedding had been the day before. The Lord gives us signs, but so often, we either don't see them, or we don't pay attention until it's too late. Anyway, I was crying so hard in my dream that I must have broken into a sweat, because, when the alarm clock went off and I awoke, the pillow was soaked.

It was a relief, though, to realize that it had only been a dream—or, rather, a nightmare. I had spent too much money on this wedding to risk missing my wedding day. I had even bought both of our rings. I did this because my husband-to-be told me that all his money was tied up. I didn't ask him why or where it was tied up. I just believed what he told me. I knew he was working on a CD at the time, so I just trusted him. It wasn't until after the wedding that I found out that he didn't have any money.

After shaking off the bad feelings of the nightmare, I got myself ready for the wedding. But then I suddenly realized that there had been no plans made to get me to the church that day. I had been so busy coordinating the arrival of the wedding party and making all the other arrangements that I'd forgotten to arrange my own transportation to the church. And that's when it hit me: my Bishop Woody had not made any plans to get me to the church either. Was this a taste of what our future marriage might bring?

Frantic, I picked up the phone and called "Old Faithful"—my brother-in-law (my sister's husband). Within forty-five minutes, we were on our way.

As we drove to the church that afternoon, my brother-in-law seemed unusually quiet. After a while, he couldn't hold his feelings back any longer. "Now if you don't want to do this, let me know," he said. "I can turn this car around, make some phone calls, and we can go the other way." To this day, we laugh about that conversation; but how right he turned out to be.

Much later, I found out what the basis was of my brother-in-law's feelings that day. He worked with some people who knew of Bishop Woody and knew the church with which he was associated. When he told these people that I was getting married to this man, people started to talk. They said all kinds of things… "Don't y'all know about that church and that bishop over there? They're all gay. And that church has been like that for many years." As

24

it turned out, the church did indeed have a reputation for homosexual behavior, whether this reputation was merited or not. Of course, my brother-in-law didn't want to believe it, thinking it was all idle gossip, but, again, how right those people turned out to be. Although he didn't believe any of it at the time, and even through my brother-in-law and I have our differences—as we all do—he felt he wanted to warn me. After all, none of us wants to see anything bad happen to another person.

The church was quite packed when we arrived. The bridal party was anxiously waiting for their cue, the organ player was poised to kick off the music, the preacher was in the pulpit, and I was ready to commit the rest of my life to this man. But the man—the groom—was missing.

After the wedding had been delayed for nearly an hour, my brother-in-law decided to check on his future brother-in-law to see what the problem was. As it turned out, the groom was locked in an upstairs room with his groomsmen… with his shirt and shoes off. He tried to get my brother-in-law to come into the room with them. My brother-in-law said, "Oh no, man… it's cool. I'll wait for y'all downstairs. So what you gon' do? My sister-in-law is downstairs, and everybody's waiting. So what's up…?"

The guests were obviously getting a little restless, so there were sighs of relief when the groom finally appeared. As the wedding march started, my brother-in-law took my arm in preparation for the march down the aisle. I couldn't help noticing the look on his face before we took our first step. He whispered in my ear, "All we have to do is turn around; I'm ready if you are." He obviously knew something that I was too blindly in love to notice, much less heed. The human being in me blocked out the spiritual signs—signs that were, in retrospect, obvious as well as timely.

Before I knew it, I was standing before the preacher, only minutes away from taking my vows. It all happened so fast. And before I knew it, I was married and standing at the front of the receiving line, accepting congratulations.

Looking back now on that October day, I realize that, in truth, I was only a character in a well-rehearsed play. When the play was over, I was left with an empty script, with only me to fill the pages. Five months after taking my vows, I would have a full understanding of what the covenant of these vows would mean. These vows were of man, not of God.

Months later, I heard about a friend who described my wedding as "a sad occasion—a funeral rather than a wedding" and about how she cried afterward. She may have cried then, but I would cry many nights to follow. For what I thought would be a beautiful beginning had ended at the start.

"I know that whatever God does, it endures forever; nothing can be added to it nor any things taken from it. And God does it so that men will [reverently] fear Him [revere] and worship Him, knowing that He is.

"That which is now already has been, and that which is to be already has been; and God seeks that which has passed by.

"Moreover, I saw under the sun that in the place of justice there was wickedness, and that in the place of righteousness wickedness was there also.

"I said in my heart, God will judge the righteous and the wicked, for there is a time appointed for every matter and purpose and for every work.

"I said in my heart regarding the subject of the sons of men, God is separating and sifting them, that they may see that by themselves under the sun, without God they are but like beasts." *(Ecclesiastes 3:14–18)*

THE MARRIAGE VOWS

"DEARLY beloved," the preacher intoned. "We are gathered here together in the sight of God, and in the face of this company, to join together this Man and this Woman in holy Matrimony; which is an honorable estate, instituted of God, a union that is between Christ and his Church. Therefore, it is not by anyway to be entered into unadvisedly or lightly; but reverently, discreetly, advisedly, soberly, and in the fear of God. Into this holy estate, these two people's presents come now to be joined. If any man can show just cause, why these two people may not lawfully be joined together, let him now speak, or else hereafter forever hold his peace."

Even though nobody said anything, there were plenty of mixed emotions in the church audience that day. There were people who didn't want the marriage to take

29

place; there were ex-girlfriends; there was my aunt who had known Bishop Woody as a child growing up; and there were some of Bishop Woody's congregants.

Then there were the people who didn't show up, because they felt that it should have been them marrying the bishop this third time. (Yes, I was to be his third wife.) When he sung to me, you should have seen the other women. "Oh bishop," they would say, as if he was singing to them and not me. Of these other people, some wanted the marriage only to get back at others. And, as crazy as it sounds, my husband-to-be was one of them. As I look back on that day, it was a performance, and when the curtains closed, it became a living nightmare.

The preacher continued, "Will you have this Woman to be your wedded wife, to live together after God's ordinance in the holy estate of Matrimony?"

Bishop Woody said, "I do."

"Will you love her, comfort her, honor her, and keep her in sickness and in health, and forsaking all others…"

Perhaps the preacher should have said, "…forsaking all others, men included."

"…keep thee only unto her, so long as you both shall live?"

"I do," he said.

"Will you have this Man to be your wedded husband, to live together after God's ordinance in the holy estate of Matrimony?"

"I do," I said, but what was I thinking?

"Will you obey him, and serve him, love, honor, and keep him in sickness and in health; and, forsaking all others, keep thee only unto him, so long as you both shall live?"

Again, I said, "I do," but, again, what was I thinking?

"Now repeat after me… 'I, Bishop Woody, take this Woman to be my wedded wife, to have and to hold from this day forward, for better or for worse, for richer or for poorer, in sickness and in health, to love and to cherish, till death us do part, according to God's holy ordinance; and thereto I plight thee my troth.'"

When Bishop Woody had finished his vows, it was my turn. The preacher turned to me and said,

"Now repeat after me… 'I, Angel, take this Man to be my wedded husband, to have and to hold, from this day forward, for better or for worse, for richer or for poorer, in sickness and in health, to love, cherish, and obey, till death us do part, according to God's holy ordinance; and thereto I give thee my troth.'"

Well, I guess I lived up to my vows… for better or worse. I stuck it out until my new husband put me out of the church. For richer or poorer… I didn't leave when I found out that he had no money. In sickness and in health… I didn't leave when I found out he was sick with the homosexual fever, which, in turn, caused his health to deteriorate. I didn't leave… I prayed. As I will pray until death us do part according to God's holy ordinance. And With this Ring I thee wed, and with all my worldly goods I thee endow… He didn't have anything, so I definitely wasn't marrying him for money. In the Name of the Father, the Son, and of the Holy Ghost. Amen.

The preacher continued, "Let us pray: Our Father who art in heaven, Hallowed be thy Name. Thy kingdom come. Thy will be done on earth, as it is in heaven. Give us this day our daily bread. And forgive us our trespasses, as we forgive those who trespass against us. And lead us not into temptation; but deliver us from evil. Amen.

"O ETERNAL God, Creator, and Preserver of all mankind, Giver of all spiritual grace, and the Author of everlasting life; send your blessing upon these, your servants, this man and this woman, whom we bless in thy Name of Jesus that they live faithfully together, so these persons may surely perform and keep the vow and covenant between them made, whereof this Ring given and received is a token and pledge, and may ever remain in perfect love and peace together, and live according to your laws; through Jesus Christ our Lord. *Amen.*

"FORASMUCH as Bishop *Woody* and *Angel* have consented together in holy wedlock, and have witnessed the same before God and this company, and thereto have given and pledged their troth, each to the other, and have declared the same by giving and receiving a Ring, and by joining hands. I now pronounce you Man and Wife, in the Name of the Father, and of the Son, and of the Holy Ghost. Amen. May the Holy Ghost bless, preserve, and keep you; and the

Lord mercifully with his favor look upon you, and fill you with all spiritual benediction and grace; that ye may so live together in this life, that in the world to come you may have life everlasting. *Amen.* You May Kiss The Bride..."

So, that was my wedding. What should have been a beautiful beginning was more of an ending. But, paradoxically, this ending would also be a new beginning, but not in a way I would have ever thought or expected. What I am about to share with you over the next few chapters changed my life forever.

IN HINDSIGHT

Before continuing with the story of my marriage, I would like to share a recollection of a one-day counseling session my soon-to-be husband and I had with one of his pastor friends. During this session, the two of them told me that the women in the church were going to "do things to me" because they wanted to be with Bishop Woody. The other pastor said that I should just remember that Bishop Woody was marrying me. You can imagine my reaction. I told the two of them that I should have had my attorney with me.

This was another learning experience. I thank God that He was with me and that the blood of Jesus Christ covered me. I could have lost my life in this marriage.

Not only this, but I will never forget my husband-to-be saying to me, "Everyone is going to think I'm marrying you because you're famous."

I thought about this for a moment and then said, "I'm not famous."

"Yes you are," he replied, "because you've been in Essence magazine."

This was another great lesson for me. We need to listen to what people say; it can tell us a lot about their motives and about where they are coming from. I mean we need to listen with our spiritual ears, not with our earthly emotions. We have to be more cautious about who we get into a relationship with and about who we end up bringing into our children's lives. I had signs, and I ignored them. I could only think about how I wanted to be married. And I thought that one couldn't get any closer to God than being married to a bishop.

This was my ignorance—the same as me thinking that Elvis was still alive on an island with Tupac and Biggie. But at the time, I was not spiritually awakened enough to recognize demons and evil spirits. In my wildest dreams, I would have never thought that a person calling himself a man of God could have treated me the way he did. But, as the Bible says, "God is no respecter of persons." I thought I had been blessed with a wonderful husband, and I still believed that he could have been. But when our life is full of sin, we are not serving God; we are serving Satan.

In retrospect, I think that my husband-to-be and I should have sought counseling with my own pastor; those evil spirits would have never gotten past my pastor. It's all very well, though, to speculate on what might or might not have happened if this or that had gone some other way. But, even if it had, would I have listened? Would I have opened my eyes to what was going on? And even if I had, would it have made me change the direction in which I was

heading?

HOW I WAS PUT OUT OF THE CHURCH
(Part One)

(The events and circumstances I share in what follows do not pertain to all ministries.)

I had never heard of anyone being put out of the church—out of the house of God—until one day, I was at a friend's house, and she told me that she wanted to talk with me. She said that she had been put out of church. I asked why. She told me it was because she and the pastor's wife had disagreed on an issue. I asked her what the issue was. As it turned out, it was over a program the church was organizing. "Couldn't you all have come to some kind of agreement?" I asked. "You didn't disrespect the pastor's wife did you? Because, at that point, you would have been wrong." My friend explained that she had not. I told her to stop joking around with me, saying that I just knew she couldn't have been put out of church for the reason she was telling me. As it turned out, though, she was serious.

Based on what I've since experienced, I'm no longer surprised when I hear stories like this. We just don't know what people are capable of until it happens to us. In my case, the spirit of homosexuality attacked my marriage, and I, too, was put out of the church. I remember that November day as though it was yesterday...

We were having a program at our church for my husband. Before this, I had gone to the salon and then home to get dressed. All the while, I was feeling weighted down by some kind of heavy atmosphere; there was something 'evil' in the air. At the time, I didn't quite know what was going on. Later, though, I understood that I was in the midst of a spiritual warfare. The demons and evil spirits were attacking me, making it very hard for me to get to the church.

When I finally reached the church, I opened the door, and one of the ladies from the church was standing there. At that moment, it all caught up with me, and I broke down crying. The lady from the church hugged me and said, "We've made it this far; just hold on." She escorted me downstairs to where the others were.

When it was time for the program to start, we went upstairs into the church. As we walked in, I saw many bishops and their wives, apostles, and pastors. Many of them were from out of town, and I could feel the spirit of homosexuality everywhere; they were flaming hot. "Help them Jesus," I said!

Then I saw my husband. He couldn't even look at me. He stepped back and hid his face; I know that he felt the God in me that day; it seemed stronger in me than any other day. Despite how weak I was at the time, God's strength was making me strong.

The program began, and the program director began introducing everyone who was participating in the event. Before going on, let me tell you something about this particular program director...

Apart from anything else, this particular program director was once a nail technician, and the organization that all the nail techs belonged to had a reputation for putting forward their own kind as bishops. Anyway, five months into my marriage, my husband went to a bishops' conference in Atlanta. I remember him calling me around midnight to tell me that he was getting ready for bed and that he would call me in the morning. Seven o'clock the next morning, something woke me up abruptly, and I found myself sitting bolt upright in bed. I called my husband in Atlanta, but there was no answer in his room. So I called one of the other ministers who had gone with him to the conference.

As it turned out, my husband was spotted sneaking down to the aforementioned program director's room that night. Although, at the time, I hadn't yet caught on to what was going on, I later found out that the man I married was also this program director's lover. Is it any wonder that my husband couldn't be faithful to his wife? In reality, he was living a lie, and so was I.

Let's pause for a moment and consider what we are dealing with here—from a woman's perspective. Suppose you've recently gotten married, or you've been married or dating someone for a while, and things start to change in your relationship. As a woman, your first thought is that your husband or boyfriend is messing around with another woman. But what if you find out that it's not a woman he's seeing, but a man. What are you going to feel? What are you going to do? Think about that for a moment.

Everything I'm sharing here is what I actually went through; but through it all, God delivered me and kept me. I don't believe that any of us—no matter who we are—can come through such things with our sanity intact unless God delivers us out of it. Furthermore, I believe, as the Bible says, that there is a season for everything under the sun, and that everything happens for a reason—our childhood, who our parents are or were, our siblings, and everything else in our lives. We just have to be willing to search deep enough to find out what that reason is. And we have to be willing to let God be our guide.

Coming back to the main story, the night's program director (former nail tech) introduced and welcomed all of the guests in the church. However, he never introduced me as the bishop's wife. He knew I was the bishop's wife.

How could he not? He was my husband's fellow bishop

and one of his closest friends. (Or should I say "closet"

friend?)

After the introductions, a lady sitting next to me—a

friend of the program director who came with the pastors

from out of town—was trying to get the program director's

attention. "Don't forget to introduce the bishop's wife," she

said. The next thing I knew, I was standing, and the

program director looked at me and said, "And you are?"

Well, I knew that the former Mr-nail-tech-slash-

bishop knew exactly who I was, and I thought he had better

quit playing church. I answered, "Bishop's wife."

"And your name is?" he asked.

"Angela [withheld]," I said. (I said my married

name, but can't mention it here for legal reasons.) At that,

all hell broke loose. My husband—a bishop who was

46

supposedly a man of God—said with an attitude, "We are

not going to have any of this today!"

THE STORY OF OUR SEPARATION

Before going on with the present story, I think it's important to mention that my husband and I were already separated at this stage, and that I had filed for divorce. Before I decided to file, my husband had told me on several occasions that he did not want to be married to me and had suggested that I file. I responded by saying, if you want it, you file. I tried to suggest ways in which we might be able to work out our conflicts—perhaps counseling. However, he seemed to be more concerned with appearing innocent to his congregation than with saving our marriage. He was set on portraying me as the guilty party—as a bad person— but God knew better. On the one hand, in public, he would tell people that he didn't want a divorce, but on the other hand, in private with me, he would deny ever saying that he wished to remain married. I eventually realized that this was his way of protecting his image amongst his

48

congregation and constituents. And so it went on... back
and forth.

In order to present the whole picture, it's important
that I relate the events that led to our separation—events
that were motivated by deceit...

After our wedding, my husband moved in with me.
Around the same time, though, my husband started
traveling frequently, which left me home alone quite a lot. I
was uncomfortable with this, particularly as there were
increasing break-ins and vandalism in the area. So we
discussed moving to a more secure neighborhood. I also
thought it more appropriate, now being married, that we
jointly lease our home; he agreed, and I started searching
for a new home.

Once I found the home I liked, shared it with him,
and he had agreed to it, I started the legal process.
However, when it came time to close the deal, my husband

refused to jointly sign the lease; he insisted that I sign alone. Not being suspicious at this stage, I complied.

I went forward with arrangements to move into our new home. During this time, my husband was traveling frequently to Chicago. On one occasion, I received a phone call from a friend of my husband who lived in Chicago. He asked me why I was moving to Novi, MI, as this was "too far away," he said. Too far away for whom? I wondered! At first, I was confused, and then I was insulted by his question. What right did he have to question me about decisions my husband and I had made about our life together? When I shared this telephone conversation with my husband, asking him if he knew the reason for the call, he pleaded ignorance. The ugly truth would come out later.

Finally, it was moving day, and my husband had returned home from Chicago. I had made all of the necessary preparations and arrangements for the move. When my husband came over that day, he asked me what I was doing, feigning ignorance. I said, "We're moving today!" He replied, "I'm not moving anywhere!"

I had no choice but to move, though; my current lease had expired and the new one had already been signed. In addition, I had put down a deposit of twenty-five hundred dollars of my own money. He never helped me with anything. What did he care? He wasn't losing anything; it was my money, not his. The whole incident was shocking to me, because we had previously discussed and agreed to move. Being husband and wife, I naturally assumed that he would be joining me in our new home. Yet, he acted as though we had never talked about it.

As it turned out, there was a premeditated design behind his actions. His intention all along was to use his obligation to the church and our marriage to conceal his homosexual relationship, thereby protecting his image—a wolf in sheep's clothing. Now, by orchestrating our separation, he would be free to continue his homosexual tendencies, misleading both his congregation and me with his masquerade of doing the work of God.

(The plot thickened later, when I found out that my husband's grandfather was also a homosexual bishop— married, but separated from his wife, and that's not all. It seems that my husband had a generational curse on his life.)

It's bad enough that my husband deceived me about his homosexuality. It's worse, though, that he was knowingly deceiving the church and his congregation. Homosexuals acting publicly as though they want to be married to women when they really do not is really just a front—in this case, a front for homosexual ministers attending to their own personal greed and gain.

Homosexual ministers know the word of God; this is how they lure and deceive people in the church. It's called artificial bait. Let's be clear about this, though; not all ministers are homosexual and not all are misrepresenting God. However, the ones who are will fool the very elect, as the Bible says. But one has to study to discern this. Their crafty words and enticing speeches make women and men believe, just as Satan did when he used crafty words to get Eve to eat from the forbidden tree. Satan is still up to his nasty ways.

In particular, these kind of men use women for whatever they can get in terms of momentary pleasures. I have first-hand experience of this; this spirit attacked my marriage and tried to ruin my life. However, when I started binding that demon up in the name of Jesus and pleading the blood, it fled. Such spirits and demons will not come out of these individuals unless the persons themselves truly wish for salvation. Unfortunately, though, some people have been caught up in sin for so long that they think it's a part of their lifestyle—a part of who they really are. It's not, though; it's the spirits and demons in them.

During our separation, and as time went on, my husband realized that some of his congregation were becoming suspicious about the events surrounding our separation. At this stage, I had already moved on with my life, after he had rejected all of my attempts at reconciliation. In an effort to suppress the questions and rumors, and to calm the climate, he came up with another scheme.

As it happened, I was waiting in the lobby of my new companion's doctor's office—when an acquaintance of my soon-to-be ex-husband and mine walked in. This acquaintance was not aware of our separation and our pending divorce. While I was waiting for my new companion, the acquaintance asked me how my husband and I were handling the commute from our respective homes in Novi and downtown Detroit, assuming that we had agreed to separate living arrangements. He assumed that we jointly had both homes, but that we used the downtown Detroit home mainly to limit the commute to the church. I corrected him, informing him that the arrangement was the result of divorce proceedings.

Afterward, as my new companion and I were leaving his doctor's office, we saw the aforementioned acquaintance (as it happened, the acquaintance was also a bishop) getting into his car and straight onto his cell phone. We found out later that this gentleman began spreading the word about the true nature of the relationship between my husband and me as soon as he left the doctor's office. It may be hard to believe, but this is really what some church folk are like.

Some time after this, I received a call from another pastor's wife. She said that my husband had asked her to call. She told me that she really felt that my husband wanted me back. I said to her, "He may fool you, but he can't fool me." However, in the end, her conversation was so convincing that I decided to return to his church. After all, I didn't want to be disobedient if this was God moving in my life.

Well, as it turned out, he had just used her! He knew that people were talking about how he had treated me and that they were saying that he deserved everything he was getting. His new scheme was to make people think that he missed me and wanted me back—once again to save his image. After hearing the rumors that were coming from his congregation, he even asked his congregation to pray for us. He told them that he was still their pastor and that I was still their first lady, and to stop their gossip, because he still loved me and wanted me back. He started to act as though this were all true; he wanted to make it look good, because he had to get me back to the church in order for his plan to work.

I remember my first Sunday back to the church after this. As I touched the door to go in, I could feel that the presence of evil spirits was strong; I could feel that they did not want me back in the church.

During this and ensuing visits to the church, my husband never asked me to move back in with him nor did he ask about my children. This told me that he was not sincere about reconciling. During these visits, he would regularly say evil things to me. For example, he told me that he didn't love me and that he didn't want to be with me. Of course, no one heard him; he would only say these things when no one was around.

Some Sundays, when I didn't come to church after being verbally abused by him, some of the congregation would ask him where I was. He would make up some kind of excuse; he constantly lied about me to his congregation and friends.

He also let a few of the people in his congregation, friends, and others hear messages that I sent him on his cell phone. In particular, he would let them hear specific messages where I was cussing him out. He made sure they didn't hear any of the other messages; he wanted to make sure they didn't know the whole story. And they weren't interested in the reasons why I was cussing him out, so, of course, they believed everything he said.

But frankly, it was none of their business. He was my husband, and whatever we did in our house was our business. I know I wasn't at the level I should have been in my spiritual life, and I shouldn't have ever stooped so low. Yes, I cussed. However, although there were a lot of things that he did that I was willing to overlook, by this time, I had had all I could take from him.

Then there was the question of his spending habits. Every week, he would ask me for money, and we're not talking about small amounts. One particular week, he asked me for two hundred and fifty dollars. I had just spent four hundred dollars or so for a robe he had ordered for the

Atlanta conference. Naturally, I started getting a little curious about what he was doing with so much money. He could never keep money; it went through his hands like water. By this time, he had also stopped taking me places; we were not going out anymore; things just started to change.

After a time, my curiosity about his spending habits got the better of me. I had obtained the code for his cell phone (which, by the way, I was also paying for). So, one day, I called his cell phone and accessed his messages. One of the messages was a girl saying, "Oh, thank you for the flowers; they're beautiful." In the background, another woman was asking the girl, "What's the occasion?" The girl replied to her, "Just because!" She went on to say (on the message), "You know who it is. Call me. And thanks again for the flowers!" There was no way that this message had anything to do with a business deal!

When I called my husband and asked him who the girl he bought flowers for was, he claimed that he didn't know what I was talking about. So, I told him to hold on and not to answer his cell phone the next time it would ring. I dialed his cell phone number from our three-way-calling at home, clicked back over to him, and let him first hear that this was his cell phone we were calling. When he agreed that this was indeed his cell phone, I entered his code, and we listened to a few of his messages. Again, he agreed that these were his messages. Then, I went forward to the message I wanted him to hear.

The first thing he said was, "I don't know who that is."

"Why did you save the message then?" I asked. "The only time we save a message is when we want to go back and listen to it again. Don't even try it!"

"I thought it was strange, and I wanted to find out who it was," he lied, "so I saved the message." Then he got angry with me and hung up the phone.

When I tried to call him back, I kept getting his voice mail. I found out later that he was changing the code on his cell phone. I threw my hands up. This was weak of him, but what did it matter? I'd had enough of him at this point.

It was apparent from this episode that my husband was misusing money—most of it mine—for his own lifestyle, while there were people in the church who needed help. He was whoring around on me and doing all kinds of ungodly things.

As if the preceding wasn't bad enough, a few months after we were married, I found out that he had been picked up by the police for prostitution a month before we met.

When I would ride with him before we were married, we would be on Mack Ave., and, one time, out of the clear blue sky, he told me that the women who were walking Mack were not prostitutes, but policewomen. I started having strange feelings when we would drive down Mack, but I wouldn't say anything. I had a feeling that he knew all about prostitution. It was strange.

One night, after being married to him for a while, I woke up out of my sleep and called him at the church. When he answered the phone, I started screaming, "Prostitutes, prostitutes!" and hung up the phone. Later, when he got home, I remember him sitting on the side of the bed and waking me up. In a calm voice, he said, "What did you mean when you called me today and said 'prostitutes'?"

I was a little drowsy and said, "I don't know... I don't want to talk about it," and I went back to sleep.

A few days later, I was looking for some paperwork in a draw where we would put all kinds of things—a junk drawer. In the drawer, I found an envelope containing papers indicating that he had been picked up for prostitution.

I thank the Lord that He had me covered! I was covered by the blood of Jesus. This was serious business. I could have caught AIDS or any number of other sexually transmitted diseases.

Whether we want to believe it or not, there are men out there who are on the "down low"—men who may be dating you, your daughters, and, God forbid, your sons. To know the spirit of the truth, we need to get into a church home, a Bible-teaching church, and study the word for ourselves.

Not too long into the marriage, my husband had stopped communicating with me. And, after only two months of marriage, he had no desire to engage in sexual relations with me. Of course, this made me suspicious. He had also been acting out of character. When he would go out of town, he would wear his wedding ring out of the house, but was evidently taking it off when he got to where he was going, as this next incident will show...

After my husband had been away one time, I got hold of his hotel room receipt. Already being suspicious about his recent behavior, I called the number on the receipt—a number that he had dialed back-to-back ten times. A young girl answered; she was about eighteen years old and, as I found out, was still living at home with her mother. We talked, and she said that my husband had tried to flirt with her. I asked her if she had noticed the wedding ring on his finger, stating that he was married. She said that she hadn't noticed a wedding ring. I asked if she knew that he was a bishop. She replied that she did not know he was a bishop and that he didn't carry himself that way.

During the call, I could hear talking in the background. Apparently, it was the girl's mother, who was listening to our conversation. She was asking her daughter who she was talking to. When her daughter told her, the mother told the daughter to hang up the phone. "You don't be talking to no other man's wife about him," she said. Without another word, they hung up on me!

During this time, my husband and I would see each other at events. At these events, other people would tell me that he would deny we were even married. He would also try to make me look bad in front of others. And all he had to do to support his allegations was to let them hear me cussing him out on his cell phone that one time. Of course, this was only one small side of the whole picture, but these others didn't know that. All in all, it showed that he could really run someone into the ground when it suited him.

All of the preceding incidents demonstrate how the enemy sits waiting for a chance to twist anything good into evil, or for a chance to cast blame on innocent actions. Beware of a scoundrel and his evil plots, as he may ruin your reputation forever. He will take your gifts and then use them to get the better of you, and you will suffer a double wrong in return for the favors you have done for him. If you wish to do a good deed, first check out the person whom you would grace with your deed; then you will have credit for your kindness. A good turn done to a God-fearing man will be rewarded—if not by him, then by the Most High God. The Most High God hates sinners and, in the end, sends bad men what they deserve. Take no pleasure in the pleasures of the wicked; remember that they will not go scot-free all their lives.

Let's now return to the part of the story where I was put out of the church—with the program director questioning who I was in front of the congregation...

HOW I WAS PUT OUT OF THE CHURCH
(Part Two)

During the church ceremony, after my husband denounced my presence, an elderly lady stood up and vouched for me, saying, "She is his wife!"

At this point, my husband sent over one of his colleagues—a certain Rev. Toy—to tell the elderly lady to shut up, because she didn't know what she was talking about. Rev. Toy then announced to the congregation, "The bishop doesn't want her anymore."

I turned and faced this demon as he began to say to me, "I hate you!"

I looked that demon in the eye and, seeing how weak he was, I said, "I bind you up in the name of Jesus and plead the blood." A lady sitting next to that demon, hearing what it had said to me, also started pleading the

67

blood of Jesus. Apparently, she could not believe what this man had said to me after I had stood up as the bishop's wife.

Sitting on my other side was a lady who was the wife of another homosexual bishop from out of town and the sister of the apostle.[2] She took my hand and said, "Baby, don't worry, I know what you're going through, and it's going to be OK." She was right, of course, because I was getting the heck out of there straight away. I refused to stay in that demonic relationship any longer.

At this point, the homosexual demons went crazy, and this lady's husband was one of them. There were demons and demonic spirits everywhere in that church. Even some of the people from my church—evangelists and ministers sitting in one of the front rows—looked as though they were in a trance. It was crazy!

---

[2] An apostle is an overseer of several churches, and head of the organization. An apostle keeps watch over the churches under his direction, to make sure everything is going according to sound doctrine.

As the program continued, Bishop Woody was walking down the aisle, showing off his garments; this was the part of the service that re-enacted his crowning as a bishop. As he walked down the aisle, I felt sick to my stomach, because he was switching more than any woman. I felt as though the world was upside down. Even the apostle said, "Walk like a man!"

After service, people were lying publicly about what had happened—even men who called themselves pastors! I knew that God had His angels around me that day, because God loves me so much that, as He says, "no weapon that is formed against me shall be able to prosper and every tongue that shall rise against me in judgment thou shalt condemn."[3] My heart danced, and I shouted right out of my jacket, because I knew at that point that God was delivering me right out of hell. The apostle even said,

---

[3] Isaiah 54:17

"That's what it looks like when the shackles are being loosed off your feet and you are freed."

I recall previously contacting this apostle—he oversaw my husband's organization—to talk about our separation and about how my husband was treating me. He was in North Carolina and asked if I wanted him to fly to Detroit to meet with us. I was afraid, though, as my husband had rejected any help I was trying to get for us. So, in the end, the apostle said he would be praying for us.

The following Sunday morning, I went to my former church. I'd had enough of demons that previous Friday night. I called my pastor's wife at home and informed her that I would be visiting their church. When the service was over, I asked her if she thought that I should go back to my husband's church.

"What did God tell you to do?" she asked.

"Nothing," I answered.

"Then, you have to go back and wait on God."

When she said that, my face dropped. I felt as though I might have passed out right in front of her. She knew that I was at my wits end and couldn't take it any longer. I was married to Satan himself, and I was sleeping with the enemy.

After these events and the conversation with my pastor's wife, I did a lot of thinking and remembering, trying to get the whole picture clear in my mind...

By this stage (and since two months into the marriage), my husband had stopped having sex with me. This was, of course, confusing for me. However, I recall an event that shone a disturbing light upon the situation. I came home from the office one day and received a phone call from my husband. He asked me how long it would be before I got home. I told him that I was almost home. Normally, I would have gotten home much later, so he probably thought that I would be another hour. In this case, though, I was only down the street.

When I got home, I went straight in and headed upstairs. Usually, I would have taken my coat off downstairs, but not this day. Our master bath had a glass shower in it. The way the shower was positioned, one could see the shower in the bathroom mirror. When I looked in the mirror, I saw my husband sexually satisfying himself—obviously not thinking about me. I recoiled, feeling sick to my stomach.

As I mentioned before, in the beginning of our marriage, my husband would leave me three days a week to take a class in Chicago (that had nothing to do with the church). The Bible says, "When a man hath taken a new wife, he shall not go out to war, neither shall he be charged with new business: but he shall be free at home one year and shall cheer up his wife which he hath taken."[4] So, one would have thought that this man of God would not have taken on new business, particularly where travel and being away from home were involved.

As it turned out, though, he was going there to be with another one of his flaming hot homosexual male friends—the one who had previously had the nerve to call me and tell me that my husband and I were moving too far away.

My husband pretended that he didn't know what his friend was up to or what he was talking about when he went on in a homosexual way. I felt that somebody had to speak to this man. I could not talk to him, though; he wasn't my friend. I felt that my husband had to talk to him about it. After all, he was seeing this man every week. In truth, all creatures flock together with their kind, and men form attachments with their own sort.

---

[4] 1st Corinthians 7:9

During this time, my husband was having more dinners and nights with this friend in Chicago than he was having with me. I started to feel that something was not right about this. I asked my husband on several occasions why he wouldn't talk to his friends—why he wouldn't tell them that, if they didn't change their homosexual lifestyle and practices, they would go to hell, as it was an abomination. He replied, "I can't help them." I understand now that he really couldn't help them, because he was one himself and was unwilling to change himself.

During this period of introspection, I was also reminded of a conversation I'd had with one of my husband's ex-girlfriends. She said to me, "You married him? Does his mother know? Was this marriage a secret? You don't know about him?"

"Know what? I asked.

"You'll find out," she replied cryptically.

Thanks sister! I guess I did find out—the hard way.

In those early months of marriage, I started hearing talk about him. Of course, I didn't want to believe what I was hearing; after all, this was my husband they were talking about. One bishop told me that some of the older homosexual pastors would tell the younger ones that they had to be homosexual for their ministries to work and grow. First, I found this unbelievable. Second, how did this have anything do to with my husband? I was blind to what was going on.

As a recently-married couple of the church, we started having more marital problems than I imagined a more worldly married couple of fifteen to twenty years might have had. I couldn't imagine where I went wrong. The only thing I could think was that there had been plenty of sinning (sex) before we had gotten married. During the unhappy moments of my marriage, I had smiled so much to keep from crying, that I felt as though my smile was glued to my face.

Also during this time, I began to realize that there were some women in the church as well as outside the church that wanted my husband—or what they thought was my husband. If it were now, I'd say to them, "You better watch out for what you pray for, because you just might get it." Not everybody can handle another person's assignments. What one person lives through might just kill another. No one knew from my outer appearance what my heart was really going through.

When I shared my predicament with my former pastor's wife, I remember her saying, "You have to talk to my husband; this is way over my head; it's demonic. I will be praying for you."

As I contemplated returning to my husband's church that Sunday for an evening service, I went home first to try to put my thoughts in order. I reflected upon the situations that had led to this point in my life, going back over them in my mind. At a certain point, though, it all overwhelmed me. I found myself crying and screaming out loud. I fell prostrate on the floor, giving myself up to the Lord and saying, "Please! Please! Help me, Jesus. I love you God with all my heart and all my soul. I need you to deliver me! Thank you, Jesus! Thank you, Jesus! Thank you, Jesus! Oh, God, thank you…"

Later, when I arrived at the church, I sat in my usual seat. The service had not yet started. As soon as one of the ministers saw me there, he slithered off to get the bishop. (There were some serious snakes in that church). As people were still coming in for the service, the bishop called me over. (I believe this was God handling this situation.)

"What are you doing here?" the bishop demanded. "Get your things and leave; I don't want you here anymore."

I said to him as calmly and pleasantly as I could, "OK, bishop."

I turned, collected my things, and started to leave the church. As I was walking, everything and everyone around me was a blur—I couldn't see them or hear them. The only thing I could see was the pathway out of the church.

Thinking that one of the other ministers had put me out (and not Bishop Woody), one of the deacons called out as I reached the door.

"You don't have to leave," he said. "Minister So-and-so, he can't do that."

"He didn't," I replied. "The bishop did."

The deacon looked confused for a moment, but then said, "We'll be praying for you." I didn't think praying for me was on the program that day.

When my husband put me out of that old, bricks-and-mortar building, it truly meant nothing. I had another church to go to—a church that I knew was filled with the spirit of the Lord. When we build a relationship with God and receive the Holy Spirit, nothing can be so deftly covered up that it will not eventually be made known to us. Yes, I was put out of church by a person calling himself a man of God, and this certainly had an effect upon my children and upon me. Nevertheless, by the grace of God and His mercy, we were safe. As God said, "His people will know His voice."

After my husband put me out of the church, I called him one last time. I asked him straight out if he was a homosexual.

Avoiding answering the question, he said, "If I am, you shouldn't want to be married to me."

"If you were not living a lie," I replied, "I would not have married you. The truth was never told to me from the beginning." Although he didn't answer the question, the answer was now clear in my mind.

Before closing out this chapter, let me share a few more events that took place earlier in our marriage. This will serve to fill in more pieces of the puzzle.

After only a few months of marriage, things had already started to change. I found that I was not being treated in a godly manner, as the wife of a bishop. And I was getting tired of hearing people rationalize it by saying, "He's still a man." Is he?

The problem is that when we continually accept excuses for sinful and bad behavior, things never change. Consider the fact that being with people that we are unequally yoked with can stop us from receiving our blessings. This man of God, as he called himself,

disrespected me as his wife and stood by while some of the

church members disrespected me, too. As my husband, he

stopped looking out for me, leaving me on my own. In a

way, though, I guess I was always on my own. In any case,

God's men don't act like this. God is Love.

Speaking of love, during this time, I also began

noticing that my husband appeared to be jealous of me. If a

man truly loves and cherishes his wife, how can he be

jealous of her? Yet, this seemed to be the case with my

husband. I first noticed it when God would wake me up in

the early mornings and talk to me. My husband must have

heard me talking, and, one time, he asked me,

"Is God talking to you?"

"Yes," I replied. "How did you know?"

"He used to talk to me…," he said. It was apparent

that he was jealous.

One day, I called him in Chicago to ask him about a dream I'd had—or maybe it was a vision. I told him some of what God had said in the dream and which scripture He had taken me to.

"God didn't say that to you," my husband responded, again obviously jealous.

I couldn't believe that a man could be so envious— so jealous—of his own wife that he would dismiss her contact with God. I never shared with him all of what God told me. God told me that He and I were going to knock down the walls of Jericho.

I asked myself why a man would go through the trouble of asking me to marry him and then give away the chance of having, and being with, a wise and good wife. If we are blessed with a wife or a husband after our own heart, then we need to hold on to them, love them, and cherish them. Conversely, we shouldn't give ourselves and our lives away to someone whom we cannot love or who cannot love us.

And we must approach this last point carefully. It's one thing to feel that one's husband is messing around with another woman, even though this is wrong. However, it's quite another thing to find out that one's husband is sleeping with another man. This one can't love us. As women, we can never compete with another man—neither should we, for many reasons.

One of the reasons is that we shouldn't want a man who wants another man. This should be reason enough, because we are talking about a sick person. It's demonic. When somebody does something unnatural—something they should not be doing—and they start to feel an outer body experience, that's demonic!

Personally, I can't imagine (or want to imagine) two big, grown, strong, athletic men together, having unnatural sex. It's beyond my comprehension. And it's sick—

definitely sick. There is no excuse for this kind of behavior,

and no one can give me one—particularly with respect to

people claiming to be men of God. It's also scary, because

they are not telling us who they are—it's all happening

behind closed doors. Nevertheless, when we get into the

spirit, all the lies, deceit, and secrecy fall away, and we can

tell who they are. The devil is a liar. And I am truly

thankful for the truth.

MOVING ON—THE AFTERMATH

I can truly say, now and even in the midst of what I went through, that I forgive each and every person, in the church and outside the church, who ever trespassed against me—every person who might have ever treated me badly, caused me pain, or lied against me. Conversely, if there is anything that I did to them or neglected to do for them that caused them pain or suffering—known or unknown to me—I hope that they will forgive me, too.

Through all my trials and tribulations during this time, I know that it was God who was keeping me. I was just a puppet on a string, and God was the puppet-master, directing my every move. I know that if it had been solely up to me, I would have drop-kicked a lot of those disrespectful church women. But all I can do now is love them all—my ex-husband included—because they have all helped me to become stronger than I was before. If it had

not been for the Lord, where would I be.

Thinking back on it now, some of those church

women were really out of order; it baffles me now how

they can think that their blessing is coming after the way

they disrespected me as the bishop's wife and first lady.

The point they were missing was that it wasn't about what

Bishop Woody and I were going through as husband and

wife at the time; it was, and is, about the individual

person's heart, thought, and actions; this is what God looks

at.

The church congregation was supposed to be

praying for us; instead, some of them were cursing us.

What they failed to realize was that, by cursing our

marriage, they were cursing themselves. The Bibles says, "I

will bless those who bless you and curse him who curses

you. [5]Throughout all their sniping, gossip, back-stabbing, and lies, I don't think they ever considered what it would have been like if it had been *them* going through what I was going through instead. The congregation was out of order.

God didn't let them get too tough and out of hand with me, though; at times, I gave it back to them exactly the way they deserved. I didn't get disrespectful, but I had to let them know where I stood; don't let the smooth taste fool you, as they say! God gave me this assignment for a very good reason; He knew I wasn't one to step lightly when it came to the kind of evil with which I was confronted.

The pastor at my former church once told me a story: a man at his job said to him, "Since you're a Christian, if I slap you, you're not going to do anything, right?"

The pastor replied, "Just know that if you decide to slap me, whatever is in me could come out."

---

[5] Gen. 12:3

In other words, when I was married and going through all those challenges, those witches at the church were pressing against my buttons, and what was in me came out. It was a Godly out, though, being as I was a puppet for Christ; He had the strings. I am a Christian, but I was a sinner first, and we all sin and fall short of the glory of God daily. This is why I had to, and still do, pray on a daily basis; it's for my own good, I know. When these women had me backed up against the wall, if I hadn't been praying and hadn't had God guiding me, no telling what might have happened—like backing a cat into a corner. Those women were evil, but even though the women in our church were evil, the root of all the evil came from their leader. Bishop Woody was the kind of person who doesn't hesitate to defraud others for personal gain. He devoted his heart to greed and didn't care about the suffering he inflicted upon others.

When men of this sort start quoting certain scriptures out of the Bible like, "It's better to marry than to burn,"[6] as my husband did before we were married, these scriptures may be true statements, but take the time to find out what the motives are behind their quoting it.

God has a plan for people like this, though; they will reap what they sow. We must all be careful that we do not become greedy and mistreat others to gain money or possessions. There were strongholds and factions in my ex-husband's church, as in other churches, driven by the spirit of haughtiness, which is pride. And, as the Bible says, "Pride goes before destruction and a haughty spirit before a fall."[7]

Every week, it was something different. One Sunday morning, we were getting ready for church. I was telling my husband that the kids (my children before my

---

[6] 1st Corinthians 7:9
[7] Proverbs 16:18

marriage to Bishop Woody) needed to stay at our home on Saturday, so they could ride to church with us instead of making two trips. We were not arguing or anything, but then, clear out of the blue, he pushed me so hard that I hit the back of the walk-in closet. At the time, he weighed 328 pounds and I weighed 128. I had no idea why he did this; I just couldn't comprehend this man's hatred for me.

Abuse comes in different forms, not just physical or sexual. Although all forms of abuse are bad, I personally feel that verbal abuse is the worst, because no one ever reports this type of abuse. No one gets prosecuted for it, although they should, I feel. People that specialize in wicked words display their abuse through their tongue. As the Bible says, "For out of the abundance of the heart the mouth speaks."[8]

When a person specializes in verbal abuse, there are no visual bruises, and they laugh afterwards. Their plan is

---

[8] Matthew 12:34

to scar the spirit, bruise the soul, and destroy the self-esteem. My husband became very verbally abusive, and I couldn't understand what was going on.

When I would ask him if he loved me, he would say, "Sometimes I do, and sometimes I don't." And this was after we had only been married for a short time. This was the man who told me that he wanted me to go everywhere he went, claiming that he would never leave me. This was the man who asked me to marry him. What was wrong with this picture? It wasn't for me to understand at the time, but I understand it now. My husband couldn't be in a lasting relationship with a woman, because he was living a homosexual lifestyle. A marriage would only last long enough for him to get what he needed: money, the appearance of respectability, a front for his otherwise disreputable behavior, and so forth.

I remember talking to some of his friends when I was trying to get counseling for us. They said that this was not the first time he had done these sorts of things; apparently, he had a tendency to marry for the wrong reasons. Incidentally, I also remember my husband telling me that one of the ladies in his singing group once asked him if he loved me. Of course, he said yes, always trying to maintain the illusion.

After we were married, my construction office was located in the downtown area. My husband and I talked about moving my office to the church so I could save some money. As it turned out, though, he was only looking for ways of getting himself more money.

The new office was off the sanctuary of the church. I brought my construction crew in to remodel—drywall, paint, lay new carpet, and so forth. The church didn't pay for it, though. I did. And that was OK. Before we were married, the church was having the basement remodeled, but ran out of money. So, this being my and my husband's church home, I was happy to do this. My construction crew painted the entire basement and fixed the lighting. I paid

the remaining balance on the carpet they had in layaway

and got that laid. I ran a new phone system throughout the

church and put a down-payment on wiring for the new

internet service.

When my husband and I were divorced, I didn't get

any of my money back. Not that I wanted it back; that

wasn't what it was all about. It was about where my heart

was. I just wanted the best for my church; after all, it was

my church home, too. So, I don't regret it. However, the

whole story illustrates my ex-husband's motivations. As the

Bible says, "A double-minded man is unstable in all his

ways." And, although the church benefited—as I did in

terms of the strength the whole experience gave me—I am

glad that part of my assignment is over.

At times, I would ask my husband questions about

the Bible and about what God says under His covenant.

One time, he replied, "It don't matter what the Bible says,

because I have done all I am going to do with the Bible." This was when I knew that it was time for me to leave. I realized that the only reason that this demon was in him was because he wanted it to stay.

Speaking of demons and as I mentioned before, research carried out during my divorce brought to light that my husband was under a generational curse of homosexuality—a curse only he has the power to break. His grandfather was a homosexual. His mother had a woman living with her who wore better suits than a man. When I would ask my husband about it, he would just ignore me.

When my husband was growing up, he played the organ for a well-known minister who was known to be a homosexual. They say that, before this well-known bishop died, he told all those around him who were practicing homosexuality that God had said for them all to stop their homosexual ways. When I would ask my husband why he wouldn't tell his friends that they would go to hell if they didn't change their ways, he would tell me that he couldn't help them. I guess he felt that he couldn't help them while he was practicing the sin himself.

HOW GOD REVEALS OUR LIVES TO US

God reveals to us what is going to happen, even before it happens. God revealed to me what was going to happen with respect to a meeting with my husband. He said that things were not going to turn out the way I wanted them to, and, sure enough, they didn't. I was forced to face the fact that this whole episode of my life was a very short assignment, and it was now coming to an end. I had put everything I had on the line to try to save my marriage. In addition, I was losing my business; I lost a twenty-six million dollar contract, and that's not all. Let me share this story...

As I mentioned previously, before I met Bishop Woody, I already owned my own construction firm. One day, I received a phone call from a contractor in Florida. He had found my information on a website for government contractors. He was looking to team up with a minority firm. As it happened, my firm was a certified, minority, female-owned construction firm and certified as a SBA 8a contractor with the government. By doing business with me, this contractor's company would get two minorities for the price of one—black *and* female.

He told me about a twenty-six million dollar contract that they were bidding on to build a 200,400 ft^2 office building in Florida. I had been praying for a contract like this for a very long time. I knew that it was time and that my dream was finally coming true. This project was going to be history for my company.

To cut to the chase, this construction firm flew me out to Florida, and we began the paper process that was going to make the deal happen. It all looked so good— almost too good to be true. I would be required to fly to Florida two weeks out of every month for the next three years. When the project was finished and all the taxes had been paid, I would come home with a grand total profit of $1.7 million. Not bad for three years of work!

In the meantime, I was married, and, after the wedding, all hell seemed too break loose. Talk about being married and unequally yoked! But that was just what was going on in my life. Then, all of a sudden, this million-dollar contract completely fell apart.

Think about all this from a spiritual perspective... I was trying to keep my marriage together, my husband had stopped having sex with me, all communication had ceased between us, and I couldn't even think straight. I was confused, to say the least—very confused. In the midst of all this, the contractor in Florida contacted me. At the last minute, he wanted me to sign over forty percent of my company to his wife, daughter, son, and five of his friends. And the contract stated that, if I became temporarily disabled, the president of his company would take over my company. On top of this, this contractor now wanted twice his share of the profits. Instead of making $1.7 million, I was now looking at coming home with only $700 thousand. Things had started going haywire.

Even before this, though (I later found out), when I had left for Florida, my husband pulled up a chair in front of his congregation one Sunday, and he proudly told them all about me going to Florida. He told them how blessed I was to secure such a huge contract there, as it was so hard for a woman in the construction business to make a success of it. (However, I realized later that his pride and excitement were not so much for me, but for what he thought he was going to get out of the deal.)

Between this and that, I was willing to give up everything to save my marriage. It may sound crazy, given the circumstances and events of the marriage, but that's where I was at—lost and confused. This should be a lesson for all of us not to let life's situations and negative people bring us down. What I didn't realize, being in the middle of it all, was that I was pregnant with my own deliverance. However, due to the pain I was going through—it was almost too much to bear—I almost forfeited God's plan for my life. I had to learn that God never hands out more than we can deal with at a given time; and then, He always gives us a way out.

Although my husband knew what was going on with regard to the Florida contract, he didn't know that I ended up turning the contract down. I was not willing to give them forty percent of my company under the terms they had set out; not only this, but it would have voided my certificate, and there are some things I just won't do for money.

My husband and I had initially agreed not to tell anyone about the contract, but he couldn't keep his mouth shut and went around bragging about how much money I was going to be making. It was no secret how money hungry my husband was. After this, the ladies of the church—the witches I mentioned before—all got together and started brewing up their magic against me and my company.

During this episode, someone shared with me the story of the woman of Samaria.[9] She had come to the well to draw water. Jesus came and asked her for a drink. She was perplexed, because he was a Jew, and she was but a lowly woman of Samaria. Then, Jesus told her all about herself; He knew that she had had many previous husbands, and that the man she was with was not her husband. He knew that she was thirsting, too—not for water, but for something more lasting, something spiritual. The only thing she truly needed was to drink from Jesus; one drink from Jesus and she would never thirst again. I realized from this that all I needed was Jesus; He was keeping me as I went through the storm.

---

[9] John 4:7-27

When the Florida contract started going bad, I tried to find other people to consult, to talk to about it, and to help me through it, but there was no one—not even my husband. After turning down the contract, I finally told my husband what had gone on between the contractor and me. Little did I know that this would cause even more hell to break loose in my marriage. My husband was ready to leave then; for him, it was simple: no money, no marriage. It soon became apparent just whom I was dealing with. A few months after telling him about turning down the contract, he put me out of the church. I'm sure he wanted to put me out sooner, but didn't want it to be too obvious.

Like the woman from Samaria, I also had a man who was not a husband in the trust, Christian sense of the word. As women, when we become successful, we tend to feel that we need a man in our life, because this is all that's missing. No one really wants to be alone. But we need to wait on God to send us the right man. We tend to get stuck in the natural when looking for a relationship, instead of seeking through the spiritual part of us. Granted, "When a man finds a wife he finds a good thing and obtains favor of the Lord."[10] However, we are also a part of that man's choice. If we see spiritually that this or that man is not the right one, then we need to trust this intuition.

In any case, it is gratifying to know that, as the story is now told, one of the men from the church said about my time up until being put out of the church, "She was a lady until the end."

I know that it was God who kept me. I just continued going to church, praising God, and letting Him direct my path. Before I knew it, God had delivered me right out of hell. He did it for me, and He will do it for each one of us; if we believe, then we will receive. Thank you, Jesus!

---

[10] Proverbs 18:22

Before God delivered me, I was driving to prayer one day, as I recall. It was the month of September—a month set aside for corporate prayer when we all came together to pray. As I was driving, I was talking to God, asking Him why I was still going to this church. It didn't seem to be doing any good, I was saying to Him, and it was definitely not helping my marriage.

The next thing I knew, it was as though someone was in the car with me. God—through the Holy Spirit—spoke to me, saying, "It will all be over in November." When this happened, I recall saying to myself, "Oh man! I have to go through all of this until the end of October?" After this, I didn't think anything more about it, and I continued on my way to church.

In the last week of September, we were in church, and the confirmation came. My husband said, "Well, God said it would all be over November 1." Well, I almost fell off the bench. All I could do to keep from falling was to say, "Thank you, Jesus!" Here was my confirmation. I shouted so loud that tears started rolling down my face. I knew that this was God talking to me. I knew the sensation in my body; it was the presence of the Lord.

God chooses whom He feels is right to get His message to His people. For this, one needs to be a willing and obedient vessel—one with ears to hear what the spirit is saying to the church. The church is in each one of us; each one of us is the church of the living God.

I knew everyone thought I was crazy, but I didn't care, because the Holy Ghost took over, and all I could say was, "Thank you, Jesus. Hallelujah…" After everything I had gone through, and considering who this man was and what his position in the church was, I couldn't understand afterward why this man had asked me to marry him only to tell me a few months later that he didn't want to be married to me anymore. It's a shame that he couldn't have lived with me first; if he had, as many people in the world do today (shacking), it would have helped him determine if he really wanted to marry me. As it was, this was definitely not the mindset of a godly man living under God's covenant. But this was how he was.

In hindsight, it looks as though he was just a cheap date; all he wanted, seemingly, was a couple of bucks. He used anyone and everyone. For example, I found out later that his car was in the name of one of the women at the church; she wanted him so bad she could taste it. He used her, but she, like so many others, obviously loved it, as she got exactly what she wanted out of the deal.

GOSSIP AND BACKBITERS IN GOD'S HOUSE

During my marriage, I was on my knees every night, warding off evil spirits. And God would protect me every night, keeping the demonic spirits at bay. Every night, I could feel the presence of the Lord from my head to my toes—as I mentioned before. After a time, things started to change, as God's plan for me was gradually revealed.

In the midst of it all, though, I had to deal with some difficult assignments. During this time, I was not honored as a wife, provided for, or protected. I was also disrespected many times by my husband's so-called best friend—a certain Rev. Toy, whom I have mentioned previously. Rev. Toy was another user. Only, in this case, he used my husband, doing whatever was necessary to get what he wanted from him. (He was only friendly with my husband when he needed something, which says it all.)

When I would tell my husband about Rev. Toy speaking to me in a disrespectful way, he would tell Rev. Toy what I had said. Then, Rev. Toy would disrespect me again. This was the same supposed Reverend friend that said at our wedding, "You married my brother; I love him, and I love you as a sister." It certainly didn't seem like it when he was disrespecting me!

Shortly thereafter, Rev. Toy started trying to stir up trouble with one of my husband's ex-girlfriends. He called me at home and said this ex-girlfriend wanted to talk to me. This was a woman who never liked me and was always trying to stir up trouble between my husband and me— before and after our marriage. This was the woman who had my husband's car in her name and who took him off the insurance (that the church was paying for!) when we got married.

It's hard to believe that women such as this exist within the walls of the church. As I found out, though, not everybody comes to church to praise the Lord. People come for many different reasons—some to look at the pastor, some to sleep, and some show up just because. As they say, "You name it; someone is there to claim it."

In any case, such women of the church had me kicked off the women's board. And my husband didn't do anything to stop them. This was a supposed man of God and his congregation—the same congregation that would call me at home, gossiping about my husband's ex-girlfriends… "Did you know that your husband used to date So-and-So?" they would ask. I would say back to them, "We all dated someone; we all have a past." Seeing all this messy devil's business going on around me, I said to them all, "Get thee behind me, Satan!"

Gossip and backbiting aside, a minister, no matter what his title is, should not be a homosexual. These people lay hands upon us, and spirits transfer. They pray for us, they counsel us, and, most importantly, they feed us our spiritual food. We have to watch whom we let lay hands on us, pray for us, counsel us, and feed our families and us our spiritual food. It's important for a Christian to be a part of a Bible-teaching ministry, but it's so much more important for us to study to show ourselves approved. We want a Holy Ghost-filled, anointed, pure-hearted pastor to lay hands on our families and us. Not a sinful, disturbed, unclean, and unrighteous person.

When I was married to this man, it was a nightmare and a living hell, and I wanted to wake up. I knew that a demon had serious control over him. We all have choices about who we want to serve, but nobody told me what I was going to go through with this man. The enemy will destroy our families, our friendships, give us problems on our jobs, and try to destroy our businesses if we let them.

Many people call themselves Christians and/or men and women of God and have been in church all their lives. They shout and dance while the preacher is preaching, and as soon as church is over, they walk right by you, nose in the air, without so much as a civil word. Maybe you don't have any of these spirits in *your* church (smile).

These are the sort of people who would talk about my husband and me behind our backs. Not only this, but many of them—the women, I mean (and men, too, probably!)—had been trying for a long time to sleep with my husband. It was bizarre to me… if you were in the church long before I had ever met Bishop Woody, and he had never married you much less gave you a second look, and I was his third wife… why would you think he would want you? And why would you want someone who obviously doesn't want you? This was just crazy to my way of thinking. Nevertheless, this was what some of them were like. Like the Miss So-and-So who disrespected me, while trying to attract my husband's attention with her enormous breasts.

In truth, the man didn't want me, them, or anyone else. Before these women hit the parking lot, the devil was all over them. They talked about the pastor and his wife, while many of them had been trying to sleep with the pastor for years. As I said before, everyone has a reason for coming to church, and some of the reasons are certainly not the right ones. Some of them even believed, in their fantasy worlds, that the pastor was really their husband, and they would roll their eyes at me as they walked past. "God told me that the bishop was my husband," they would say. (This happened to me on more than one Sunday.) It didn't seem to matter to them that the man was already married!

It amounts to the same thing as being used in a way where you know you are being used. Like putting the pastor's car in your name, because you think it will bring you closer to him. And this seems not to be limited to just single women, but affects married women, too. When some of these women from the church were married, they did more for the pastors than for their own husbands, if you know what I mean! When their husbands got tired of them not taking care of the home, they divorced them, because they just didn't want to listen. Then, these women developed an attitude and started blaming their husbands for everything that went wrong, ignoring or denying all that they had done or not done at home. After the divorce, now they wanted the pastor, even when it was obviously not going to happen. All I can say is, "Repent!"

Coming back to the question of gossip, though, some of these people had been in the church all their lives, saying that they were coming for the word. The word obviously hadn't hit them yet. Which word were they coming for, anyway? The preachers' message led by the Holy Spirit or the message—the gossip—they were delivering and receiving? They hadn't even grown up enough to help look after the babies (the newcomers). This was left to the pastor to do, but that's another book.

They certainly had some growing up to do. Some hadn't been to church in months, but, as soon as they heard some gossip, they would show up, making up stories and lies about what they supposedly saw or heard. In the meantime, they had their own messy marriages going on at home. And then they wondered why their husbands were cheating on them and why their health was so bad. They really needed to do themselves a favor and repent!

Some would befriend me, acting as though they were concerned about what I was going through and telling me about things that my husband supposedly did to them. In truth, they just wanted to see who had the juicy gossip. And word from the first lady... that was the juiciest! The first thing they would do after talking to me was to go and tell my husband everything, hoping to score brownie points.

I had their number after a while; I began to see right through the mess. That was why I was on my knees praying and talking to God every day. Those church woman were nothing one should play around with; the demons needed to be rebuked and how! We need to put on the full armor of God, so we can withstand the wiles of the devil. When I talk about rebuking demons, I'm talking about the spirits that people let control them.

These women were so busy through the week, keeping their gossip moving around, that they had no room left in their lives to receive their blessing from the word of God. They thought gossiping made them popular—in our church as well as in other churches, which is why our church business was everywhere. These people were more effective then the Detroit News, Free Press, or any gossip columnist. Every time they opened their mouths, it was like that old E.F. Hutton commercial. Everyone would stop and listen!

The sad part was that, although everyone knew what snakes these gossipers were, people would listen anyway. Backbiters. Listening to such gossip, knowing that it's not right, but not saying to the gossipers that it's not right is just as sad. Unfortunately, it says a lot about the kind of people they are.

It's worse, though, for supposed men and women of God to partake of such behavior. For the ministers who counsel people and then break that confidentiality, again, all I can say is, "Repent!" My husband was one of these gossipers. He would divulge everybody's business without shame or remorse. This is where his congregation got it from, too, him being their spiritual feeder.

I recall an instance of my husband breaking the confidentiality of our marriage. Another bishop from out of town had come to visit us. While I was standing there, without qualms or reservation, he told my husband that he wanted a wife just like me.

After the first visit, this bishop would call our home and ask my husband to let him talk to me. I knew this man had a thing for me, so, when he called, I would indicate to my husband that I didn't want to talk to him. Despite this, my husband would still tell this man, "Hold on. Here she is." This made no sense to me.

Shortly after this, though, is when we started having marital problems, as I mentioned before. I needed someone to talk to, but trying to find a minister to talk who was not a homosexual was difficult. Eventually, I decided to call the aforementioned bishop from out of town. Let's call him, 'Bishop Straight'; I knew he was straight, because I ended up having an affair with him. After not being able to find anyone to talk to, I called Bishop Straight, crying my heart out about my marriage. I told him that I loved my husband, but that he didn't want me. I didn't know what to do. It was then that he told me that my husband had told him that he and I were having marital problems. And he had told

Bishop Straight at a time when I didn't even know we were having problems. My husband was already telling people this. I couldn't believe it. So much for confidentiality.

Bishop Straight kept inviting me to come and stay with him for a few days so we could talk all about it. I was very vulnerable at the time. Without saying too much more, let me say that it's not wise to go somewhere like this when we are vulnerable; it can get us into trouble.

In any case, confidentiality amongst family members should be sacred. What family members tell each other in the privacy of their own homes and in their relationships should stay confidential to the grave. Particularly when one is seeking some positive guidance. It's not for them to gossip about what is going on behind closed doors, and especially not your own home. This is not spiritual.

This is why congregational worship is so important;
it breaks strongholds, cliques, and gossip circles.
Congregational worship is certainly important. However,
the gathering of people without the presence of God is a
pointless exchange of religious rhetoric, human interests,
and confused, unintelligible language that does not bring
life. It is completely ineffective. The reason so many
members of the church are still in poverty, can't get a
breakthrough, and/or have health problems, but claim they
know the word of God, is because they don't have an
intimate relationship with God.

Your pastor is not God; he is the messenger. We
need to put our trust in the Lord. If we read and study the
word of God for ourselves, we can try the spirit by the
spirit and get our breakthrough, our healing, and our
prosperity. This is the only way that we can become party
to God's will for us. Our faith will only operate to the
degree that we know and understand God's word. We

cannot act out on a breakthrough, healing, or windfall if we don't know God's word to act out on it. The only way we can become a doctor is to study and pass the exams, go through our internship, and get our degree. It's the same way with God. We must know God's word in order to experience His power.

Ultimately, we all are striving for perfection, and the church is a place where we can work toward this perfection—a place where people are delivered and their souls can be saved for everlasting life. It's a place where we can go to share fellowship with one another, where we can touch and agree in Jesus' name, but, first and foremost, it is a place where we can be blessed with the word of God. When God releases us from bad situations, but we decide to stay in them anyway, we are asking for trouble. I had to go back to the church for God to deliver me. In hindsight, I now realize that it was all a plan and part of the divine order.

HOW IT ALL STARTED

THE BIBLICAL PERSPECTIVE

Introduction

"From the beginning of the creation God made them male and female, for this cause shall a man leave his father and mother and cleave to his wife and they twain shall be one flesh: so then they are no more twain, but one flesh. What therefore God hath joined together, let no man put asunder."[11]

When a man asks for a woman's hand in marriage, it is an indication that the player in him (his roaming, on-the-prowl, sexual nature) is dead; or, at least, it should be. Similarly, for a woman who accepts to marry a man, the

---

[11] Mark 10:6-9

player in her should also be dead. Jesus said, "Follow Me and let the dead bury the dead."[12]

What happens, though, if, after you marry a man, the player in him is still alive and kicking? What if he takes it as open season for him to be a bona fide old player—and a broke one, too, who is living off you? As times goes by, we begin to realize exactly what we have gotten ourselves into. Then, knowing what we are now dealing with, the question then becomes, "Is it too late?"

Let's be totally honest and real about this, because the truth will set us all free. God gives us signs, letting us know beforehand whether we should marry a person or not. However, sometimes we let our flesh get in the way, and we do what we want to, ignoring God's signs. As the Bible says, "Watch and pray, that ye enter not into temptation: the spirit indeed is willing, but the flesh is weak."[13]

---

[12] Matthew 8:22
[13] Matthew 26:41

"Abraham rose up early in the morning and saddled his ass (donkey) and took two of his young men with him, and Isaac his son, and clave the wood for the burnt offering, and rose up, and went unto the place of which God had told him."[14] The scripture goes on to tell how God tested Abraham's commitment by commanding him to slay his son, Isaac, as an offering. (God saves his son in the end, satisfied with his commitment.) If God tested Abraham in this way, doesn't this tell us that He is testing us, too? We had better know when God is testing us; otherwise, we might just miss out on our blessing while waiting to hear from man when God has already spoken.

One thing I do know from experience is that it's not over until God says it's over. How many of us have failed our test with God by putting more trust in man than in God? Sometimes, even knowing that God has spoken a word to us—even when confirmation comes from someone

---

[14] Genesis 22:3

who doesn't know what God has said to us—we still refuse to listen to Him. What are we waiting for? What is the source of our reluctance and our failure to listen to, and heed, God's word?

In order to understand how my situation came about (and how so many similar situations come about for so many others), let me share a little biblical history. This will help us understand the biblical perspective on much of what I went through (and what many others have gone through and are going through even as we speak), plus a lot more. In addition, it will give us the basis of the true meaning of Holy Matrimony. Bear with me, as some of the following will be familiar to many of you, but not so familiar to others.

In the Beginning

"...God created the heaven and the earth,[15] the light and the darkness and God divided the light from the darkness. He called the light Day, and the darkness Night, and the evening and the morning were the first day."[16] Then God made the firmament (the expanse of the sky) and divided the waters from the waters (meaning above and below), and called the firmament Heaven. He said, let the waters under the Heavens be collected into one place of standing, and let the dry land appear and the accumulated waters, He called Seas.

God brought forth vegetation: plants yielding seed according to their own kinds and trees bearing fruit in which was their seed, each according to its kind, and God saw that it was good. God said, let the waters bring forth abundantly and swarm with living creatures, and let birds

---

[15] Genesis 1:1
[16] Genesis 1:4-5

fly over the earth, and every living thing had its own kind, and so forth.

This is a familiar picture to most of us. Now watch what God does next. After God completed everything under the Heavens and on the earth, He said, "Let us (meaning the Father, Son, and Holy Spirit) make man in His own image." In His image, God created he him; male and female created he them, to rule over everything on the earth. And God blessed them, and God said unto them, "Be fruitful, and multiply, and replenish the earth, and subdue it: and have dominion over every living thing that moves upon the earth, but of the tree of the knowledge of good and evil, thou shall not eat of it: for in the day that thou eat thereof thou shall surely die."

The heavens and the earth were finished, and all the host of them. And on the seventh day God ended His work which he had created, and God blessed the seventh day, and set it apart as His own, because God rested from all His work on that day, which He had created and made.

However, there were a couple of things that had not yet happened. God had not yet caused it to rain upon the earth, and there was not a man to till the ground. All of a sudden, there went up a mist (fog, vapor) from the earth, and watered the entire face of the earth, and the Lord God formed man of the dust of the ground, and breathed into his nostrils the breath of life, and man became a living soul.

The Lord God planted a garden toward the east in Eden, and there He put man whom He had formed to tend, and guard, and keep it. I truly believe that Eden was a beautiful place—a place where all of us would have liked to have lived and called home. Everything at that time was, as God said, good, fitting, and pleasant, and He approved of it.

A Help Meet for Adam

"The Lord God said, 'It is not good that the man should be alone; I will make him a help meet for him [someone who is suitable, adapted, and complementary for him].' After God formed every beast of the field; and fowl of the air, and God brought them to Adam to see what he would call them, and that was their names."[17]

But there was still something missing; there was not yet found a help meet for Adam. So, watch what God did… God caused a deep sleep to fall upon Adam, and while he slept, God took one of Adam's ribs from his side, and closed up Adam's side with flesh. From that rib, God made he a woman, and brought her to the man. When Adam laid his eyes upon her for the first time, he said, *"This is now bone of my bones, and flesh of my flesh: she shall be called Woman, because she was taken out of Man."* This first Woman was the most beautiful woman the world has ever

---

[17] Genesis 2:18-19

known—not just for the beauty of her face and the form of her body, but because she reflected the divine perfection of God's perfect creation. And then God said, "Therefore shall a man leave his father and his mother, and shall cleave unto his wife: and they shall be one flesh."[18] Then, God gave Adam and his new help meet dominion over the earth and all the creatures on it.

From the preceding, we now understand that God's plan for marriage consists of one male and one female, destined to become "one flesh," united physically and spiritually. This clear instruction also excludes adultery, polygamy, homosexuality, immoral living, and unscriptural divorce. "What therefore God hath joined together, let not man put asunder."[19] In other words, marriage falls under God's laws, not the laws of men. "And I say unto you, whosoever shall put away his wife, except it be for fornication, and shall marry another, committeth adultery:

[18] Genesis 2:24
[19] Matthew 19:4

and whoso marrieth her which is put away doth commit adultery."[20] What could be clearer? What could be deeper? God created family—meaning a single man and a single woman bonded together and destined to "go forth and multiply"—even before He created the church.

The Mother of Sin

Adam gave his wife the name, Eve. Then, she became the mother over every living thing on earth. Eve was a woman of unique distinction, because she was the first in so many ways. She was the first woman to live upon earth, the first woman to be called wife, the first and only woman born without sin, the first dressmaker, the first to receive the divine prophecy of the cross, the first mother to have a son who was a murderer, and the first woman to be attacked by Satan.

---

[20] Matthew 19:9

Being the first woman on earth, Eve inherited no
sin; she was pure and holy, created sinless. Yet she became
the first sinner of the world and introduced sin to her
offspring. Since then, everyone is born in sin, and shaped in
iniquity. "So I find it to be a law (rule of action of my
being) that when I want to do what is right *and* good, evil is
ever present with me *and* I am subject to its insistent
demands."[21] Created with innocence, a sinless perfection,
and endowed with all fullness of gifts of body, mind, and
soul, rich in blessings and without spot or blemish, Eve yet
sinned and caused Adam to sin. "For Adam was first
formed, then Eve. It was not Adam who was deceived, but
[the] women who was deceived and deluded and fell into
transgression. Nevertheless, [the sentence put upon women
of pain in motherhood does not hinder their souls'
salvation, and] they will be saved [eternally] if they
continue in faith and love and holiness with self-control,

---

[21] Romans 7:21, Amplified

[saved indeed] through the Childbearing or by the birth of the divine child."[22] So it was that paradise—created from the hands of God with unmatchable grace and favor—was surrendered for the world of thorns and thistles.

The Transgression

Before Eve's creation, sin was not known to Adam. Nor was it known to Eve in the beginning, even through she knew of the tree (of the knowledge of good and evil) that stood in the midst of the garden.

Of this tree, God said, "You shall not eat of it, neither shall you touch it, lest you die."[23]

But the serpent said to the woman, "You shall not surely die, for God knows that in the day you eat of it your eyes will be opened, and you will be like god, knowing the

---

[22] 1 Timothy 2:13-15, Amplified
[23] Genesis 3:3

difference between good and evil and blessing and calamity."[24]

When Eve saw that the tree was good for food, pleasant to the eyes, and a tree to be desired to make one wise, she saw nothing wrong. It was a masterpiece of suggested sin (this was the flesh working), contrived by Satan. The serpent did not tell her to sin, but insinuated in a clever and crafty way that there was nothing to worry about in eating from the forbidden fruit.

When Eve ate from the tree, she also gave some of the forbidden fruit to her husband, Adam, and he ate it also. Thus were their eyes opened, and they knew that they were naked. They then began to sew fig leaves together to make themselves aprons; this is how Eve became the first dressmaker.

Shortly after, as they walked in the garden in the cool of the day, Adam and his wife heard the voice of the

---

[24] Genesis 3:1-6, King James & Amplified

Lord God, and they hid themselves from His presence amongst the trees of the garden. And the Lord God called unto Adam and said, "Where art thou?"

And Adam said, "I heard your voice in the garden and I was afraid because I was naked and I hid myself."

And God said, "Who told you that you were naked? Hast thou eaten of the tree, whereof I commanded thee that thou should not eat?"

Adam and Eve were in some serious trouble just about now. They had eaten from the forbidden tree, and the sin was starting to kick in. Watch how Adam blames Eve and God himself...

Adam said, "The woman whom thou gavest to be with me, she gave me of the tree and I did eat."

And God said unto the woman, "What is this that thou hast done?"

And the woman said, "The serpent beguiled, cheated, outwitted, and deceived me, and I did eat." God was rather upset about now, as one might imagine, and He started setting out the curses.

The Lord God said unto the serpent, "Because thou hast done this, thou art cursed above all cattle, (domestic) animals, and above every beast (wild) of the field: upon the belly you shall go, and you shall eat dust and what it contains all the days of your life. And I will put enmity between you and the woman and between your offspring and her offspring: He will bruise and tread your head underfoot, and you will lie in wait and bruise His heel."[25]

To the woman, Eve, He said, "I will greatly multiply your grief and your suffering in pregnancy and the pangs of childbearing: with spasms of distress you will

---

[25] Genesis 3:14-15

bring forth children; yet your desire and craving will be for your husband, and he will rule over you."[26]

And to Adam He said, "Because you have listened and given heed to the voice of your wife, and have eaten of the tree of which I commanded you saying, you shall not eat of it, the ground is under a curse because of you: in sorrow and toil shall you eat of the fruits of it all the days of your life. Thorns also and thistles shall it bring forth for you, and you shall eat the plants of the field. In the sweat of your face shall you eat bread until you return to the ground for out of it you were taken: from dust you are, and to dust you shall return."[27] In short, God blamed Adam, as head of the family (husband), for not taking charge.

After this, Adam and Eve were put out of the garden, and God sent Adam to till the ground from which he was taken. And God placed at the east of the Garden of

---

[26] Genesis 3:16
[27] Genesis 3:17-19

Eden the cherubim and a flaming sword, which turned

every way to keep and guard the way to the tree of life.

Good Seed, Bad Seed – Cain and Abel

"Adam lay with his wife Eve, and she became

pregnant and gave birth to Cain. She said, 'With the help of

the LORD I have brought forth a man.' Later she gave birth

to his brother Abel. Abel kept flocks, and Cain worked the

soil. In the course of time Cain brought some of the fruits

of the soil as an offering to the LORD. But Abel brought

fat portions from some of the firstborn of his flock. The

LORD looked with favor on Abel and his offering, but on

Cain and his offering He did not look with favor. So Cain

was very angry, and his face was downcast. Then the

LORD said to Cain, 'Why are you angry? Why is your face

downcast? If you do what is right, will you not be

accepted? But if you do not do what is right, sin is

crouching at your door; it desires to have you, but you must

master it.' Now Cain said to his brother Abel, 'Let's go out to the field.' And while they were in the field, Cain

attacked his brother Abel and killed him."[28]

When Cain became jealous, and lost his mind,

killing his brother Abel, that is when Eve became the

mother of the first murderer. This came behind Eve, being

betrayed by the serpent. Satan took control of the serpent

and used it as an instrument in his work of temptation.

Jesus said in John 8:44, "Ye are of your father the devil,

and the lusts of your father ye will do. He was a murderer

from the beginning, and abode not in the truth, because

there is no truth in him. When he speaketh a lie, he

speaketh of his own: for he is a liar, and the father of it."

After Cain murdered his brother Abel, Adam lay

with his wife again, and she gave birth to a son and named

him Seth, saying, "God has granted me another child in

place of Abel, since Cain killed him."[29] At that time, men

---

[28] Genesis 4:1-8 NIV
[29] Genesis 4:25

138

began to call on the name of the LORD. Through Seth, the spiritual lineage was maintained. As Eve buried her son Abel, she saw the fruit of her sin.

After Eve confessed her sin, she heard the Lord say to the serpent, the devil, "I will put enmity between thee and the woman, and between thy seed and her seed; it shall bruise thy head, and thou shalt bruise his heel."[30]

With this first promise of the Redeemer, there began the highway that ended at the cross where Christ, born of a woman, provided a glorious victory over sin and the devil. The Bible says, "Behold, a virgin shall be with child, and shall bring forth a son, and they shall call his name Emmanuel, which being interpreted is, God with us."[31] Through a woman, God's universe became a world of sinners, lost and ruined by the fall. Now through a woman, a perfect salvation has been provided for a sinning

---

[30] Genesis 3:15
[31] Matthew 1:23

race. Through Eve's sin, death entered the world, but at the

cross, both sin and death were conquered. Through Jesus'

suffering and agony, this provided redemption for fallen

humanity. His work of redemption stood completed; He

bore the punishment for our sins and opened the way of

salvation for all. "To this end was I [Christ] born, and for

this cause came I into the world, that I should bear witness

unto the truth."[32] "But rather what we are setting forth is a

wisdom of God once hidden [from the human

understanding] and now revealed to us by God [that

wisdom] which God devised and decreed before the ages

for our glorification [to lift us into the glory of His

presence]. None of the rulers of this age or world (Satan's

people) perceived and recognized and understood this, for

if they had, they would never have crucified the Lord of

glory. But, on the contrary, as the Scripture says, 'What eye

has not seen, and ear has not heard, and has not entered into

---

[32] John 18:37, Amplified

the heart of man [all that] God has prepared [made and keeps ready] for those who love Him [who hold Him in affectionate reverence, promptly obeying Him, and gratefully recognizing the benefits He has bestowed].'"[33] "Every one that is of the truth hears my voice." [34]

When Jesus cried, "It is finished," He meant that the serpent's head, representing power and authority, had been bruised. He laid hold of all satanic principalities and powers that Eve's transgression brought into the world and put them under His feet.

As we leave our reflection upon the world's first woman, first wife, first sinner, and first mourner, there are some lessons to be gleaned from her record; for instance, many daughters of Eve have discovered that the serpent is never more dangerous than when he professes to be someone who is interested in nothing but her advancement

---

[33] 1 Corinthians 2:7-9
[34] John 18:37

in life and her welfare. What a subtle and cruel deceiver the devil is, and how ignorant so many of us can be of his devices!

Furthermore, temptation is a universal experience, and what each of us should learn from the first person on earth to be tempted, is a manner of approach and steps; we need to safeguard ourselves from a fall through the appropriation of Christ's own victory over the enemy. There is no sin in being tempted; the only sin is when we yield to temptation; by refusing to yield to the enticement of sin, our Garden of Eden remains inviolate. At the heart of this story is the moral lesson that a woman has the power for ruin or to be a blessing over a man's life, and if she falls, man falls with her. Two cannot walk together, unless they have agreed to do so.

The Covenant and Covet Relationship

Many generations after Adam and Eve, God sent a flood upon the earth and destroyed every human being, except Noah and his family. Even with a new beginning, man fell into disobedience again, and God was grieved. God wanted a people who would love and trust him as the Father. He brought this about by establishing a covenant between a chosen national and Himself. God appeared to a man name Abram (later renamed Abraham by God) and asked him to leave his country, his people, and go into a land that He would show him. Now, how many of us would pick up and leave everything and everyone, giving up our old ways and life, to go into a country that God would show us, because God ask us to? "For whosoever will save his life [the lower life] shall lose it [the higher life]: and whosoever will lose his life [the lower life] for my sake shall find it [the higher life]."[35]

God gave us a fresh start by making a covenant with Abram and allowing him to become the father of many nations of a chosen people who would become the family of God and heirs of all His possessions. He (Abram/Abraham) staggered not at the promise of God through unbelief; but was strong in faith, giving glory to God, and being fully persuaded that what he had promised, he was able also to perform. As he and his people would trust, obey, and have faith in a daily walk with God, so God would extend His love, mercy, and blessings upon them.

We could go to many scriptures in the Bible that demonstrate how Abraham and Sarah lived by faith and trusted God's word. However, let's ask ourselves, how are we to live by faith and trust God's word? This is the crux of the matter and worth thinking deeply about. For if God 1)

---

[35] Matthew 16:25

spared not the angels that sinned, but cast them down to hell and delivered them into chains of darkness to be reserved unto judgment, 2) spared not the old world, but saved Noah, the eighth person, a preacher of righteousness, bringing in the flood upon the world of the ungodly, and 3) turned the cities of Sodom and Gomorrah into ashes, condemned them with an overthrow, making them an example unto those that after should live ungodly, and delivered just Lot, who was vexed with the filthy conversation of the wicked, then what do we think God is going to do to the ungodly today?

When we enter into a covenant relationship with our mate, it is not something to take lightly. Not only are we in a covenant relationship or contract with our mate, but we are also in a covenant, contract relationship with God. Abraham and Sarah had many struggles believing God for what He had promised them, just as we do today. It is our doubt and unbelief that cancel out our faith, and we have to be very careful about that. "Yet those who marry will have physical and earthly troubles and I [God] would like to spare you that."[36] The Bible also says, "Wives, submit yourselves unto your own husbands, as unto the Lord."[37] And, "For the husband is the head of the wife, even as Christ is the head of the church and he is the savior of the body."[38]

Where we mess up is when we covet our neighbor's stuff. The Bible says, "You shall not covet your neighbor's house, your neighbor's wife, or his manservant, or his maidservant, or his ox, or his donkey, or anything that is your neighbor's."[39]

I'm sure we have all met someone who wanted everything that we had. Such a person is so busy trying to get what God has given to us that they can't receive what God has for them. That's what "covet" means; you cannot

---

[36] 1 Corinthians 7:28
[37] Colossians 3:18
[38] Ephesians 5:23
[39] Exodus 20:17, Amplifed

covet another person's relationship, house, car, business, or success and remain aligned with God. What is given to others (by God's grace) is for them, and what is given to you is for you. We need to stop being jealous of another person's success, so that God can open the door for us. We can only covet what is ours. We need to know what is for us.

As the Bible says, "And He said to them, 'Guard yourselves and keep free from all covetousness [the immoderate desire for wealth, the greedy longing to have more]; for a man's life does not consist in, *and* is not derived from, possessing overflowing abundance *or* that which is over and above his needs.' Then He told them a parable, saying, 'The land of a rich man was fertile *and* yielded plentifully. And he considered *and* debated within himself, "What shall I do? I have no place [in which] to gather together my harvest." And he said, "I will do this: I will pull down my storehouses and build larger ones, and

there I will store all my grain *or produce* and my goods.
And I will say to my soul, 'Soul, you have many good
things laid up, [enough] for many years. Take your ease;
eat, drink, *and* enjoy yourself merrily.'" But God said to
him, "You fool! This very night they [the messengers of
God] will demand your soul of you; and all the things that
you have prepared, whose will they be?"' So it is with the
one who continues to lay up *and* hoard possessions for
himself and is not rich [in his relation] to God [this is how
he fares]."[40]

---

[40] Luke 12:15-21, Amplified

HUSBANDS, WIVES, AND MARRIAGE IN THE EYES OF GOD

What is a Husband in the Eyes of God?

"One that ruleth well his own house, having his children in subjection with all gravity."[41]

"Husbands, love your wives, even as Christ also loved the church, and gave himself for it; That he might sanctify and cleanse it with the washing of water by the word, That he might present it to himself a glorious church, not having spot, or wrinkle, or any such thing; but that it should be holy and without blemish."[42]

God's word never comes back void, no matter what it looks like, smells like, or acts like. As the Bible says, "...Because the LORD hath been witness between thee and the wife of thy youth, against whom thou hast dealt

---

[41] 1 Timothy 3:4
[42] Ephesians 5:25-27

treacherously: yet is she thy companion, and the wife of thy

covenant."[43] "For the Lord, the God of Israel, says: I hate

divorce *and* marital separation and him who covers his

garment [his wife] with violence.[44] Therefore keep a watch

upon your spirit [that it may be controlled by My Spirit],

that you deal not treacherously *and* faithlessly [with your

marriage mate]."[45]

Do we think that by divorcing our partner and

remarrying another that the grass is going to be greener on

the other side? God does not favor divorce unless

fornication, adultery, a hardened heart, or abuse have

played a role. God is Love, and, as He says, "When a man

finds a wife, he finds a good thing and obtains favor of the

---

[36] Malachi 2:14

[44] Author's note: Meaning, God hates divorce that is initiated for selfish purposes; this kind of divorce is like one covering "violence with his garment," indicating that unjust divorce is equal in God's sight to cruelty and murder. Many men are being unfaithful to their wives whom they had married when they were young; they seek divorce only to marry someone else. God hates this, because when He joined them together, man and woman, they became one in the sight of God. Because of their selfishness, God turns His back on the transgressors and refuses to hear their prayers.

[45] Malachi 2:16 Amplified

Lord."[46] Why are the vows between man and woman not taken seriously anymore? Why do we refuse to kick the devil out of our marriages?

When we get married, God becomes a witness between a husband and wife. He makes a man and a woman one [flesh]; and the reason for God making two into one is because God seeks a godly offspring [from your union]. Therefore, as God says, take heed, and deal not treacherously or faithlessly with your wife (or husband, for that matter); because, if this happens, we hinder the prayers between God and us.

Marriage is a blessing from God. The Bible says, "Two are better than one; because they have a good reward for their labor. For if they fall, the one will lift up his fellow; but woe to him that is alone when he falleth; for he hath not another to help him up. Again, if two lie together, then they have heat: but how can one be warm alone? And

---

[46] Proverbs 18:22

if one prevail against him, two shall withstand him; and a threefold cord [God is standing with the two] is not quickly broken."[47]

"It is better to not make wedding vows before God, than to make the vow and not carry it out. God has no pleasure in fools. Do not allow your mouth to cause your body to sin, and do not say before the Angel [the messenger, the priest] that it was an error or mistake. Why should God be [made] angry at your voice and destroy the work of your hands? Live joyfully with the wife whom thou lovest all the days of the life of thy vanity which he hath given thee: under the sun, all the days of thy vanity: for that is thy portion in this life, and in thy labor which thou takest under the sun."[48]

A man should wait on the Lord to give him a wife of His choice, when God feels he is ready to receive her.

---

[47] Ecclesiastes 4:9-12
[48] Ecclesiastes 5:4-18, Amplified

The wife that God will give is the woman spoken of in Proverbs 31—the virtuous woman. A man has to be ready for her, because she's not just for anyone. She is the queen, Ester, who saved her nations; she is Deborah, the warrior, who went with ten thousand men and her husband up against Sisera, captain of Jabin king of Canaan, on behalf of the children of Israel. This woman is fit for a King. "Her price is far above rubies and the heart of her husband doth safety trust in her... ...She will do him good and not evil all the days of her life... ...Her children arise up, and call her blessed; her husband also, and he praiseth her. Many daughters have done virtuously, but thou excellest them all. Favor is deceitful, and beauty is vain: but a woman that feareth the Lord, she shall be praised."[49]

Lastly, God says of a husband, "When a man is newly married, he shall not go out with the army or be

---

[49] Proverbs 31:10-30

charged with business: he shall be free at home for one year and shall cheer his wife whom he has taken."[50]

What is a Wife in the Eyes of God?

"The heart of her husband trusts in her confidently and relies on and believes in her securely, so that he has no lack of [honest] gain or need of [dishonest] spoil. She comforts, encourages, and does him only good as long as there is life within her."[51]

"Who can find a virtuous woman? For her price is far above rubies."[52] Let's be clear about this: A virtuous woman is not just for any man. The man who finds himself a virtuous woman has to be a King, because she is definitely a Queen; they were both born for royalty.

---

[50] Deuteronomy 24:5
[51] Proverbs 31:11,12, Amplified
[52] Ecclesiastes 31:10

"Married women, be submissive to your *own* husbands [subordinate yourselves as being secondary to and dependent on them, and adapt yourselves to them], so that even if any do not obey the Word [of God], they may be won over not by discussion but by the [godly] lives of their wives, when your husband observe the pure and modest way in which you conduct yourselves, together with your reverence [for your husband; you are to feel for him all that reverence includes: to respect, defer to, revere him-to honor, esteem, appreciate, prize, and in the human sense, to adore him, that is, to admire, praise, be devoted to, deeply love, and enjoy your husband]. Let not yours be the [merely] external adorning with [elaborate] interweaving and knotting of the hair, the wearing of jewelry, or changes of clothes; But let it be the inward adorning *and* beauty of the hidden person of the heart, with the incorruptible *and* unfading charm of a gentle and peaceful spirit, which [is not anxious or wrought up, but] is very precious in the sight

of God."[53]

"Even as Sarah obeyed Abraham, calling him lord:

whose daughters we are, as long as we do well, and are not

afraid with any amazement."[54] "In the same way you

married men should live considerately with [your wives],

with an intelligent recognition [of the marriage relation],

honoring the woman as [physically] the weaker, but

[realizing that you] are joint heirs of the grace (God's

unmerited favor) of life, in order that your prayers many

not be hindered *and* cut off. [Otherwise you cannot pray

effectively]."[55]

With God in our lives, He will give us the wisdom,

knowledge, understanding, and discernment that we will

need for a long-lasting marriage. And as for us women,

God gives us signs; we have to start recognizing these signs

---

[53] 1 Peter 3:1-5, Amplified
[54] 1 Peter 3:6
[55] 1 Peter 3:7, Amplified

instead of ignoring them. We have to stop acting so desperate in order to be with a man. When it's time, God will send the right man, and we will know. We need to stop looking around.

Many of us (women) have been very disappointed with some of our relationships, and we have jumped right into another relationship before we have received healing. We have to cleanse ourselves of old relationships, especially if they were abusive in any way, and the only way we can do this is to be in closed fellowship with God. By the cleansing and the renewing of our souls, God can make us into the beautiful Queens that He wants us to be, but we have to go through the Lord. As was quoted before, "When a man finds a wife, he finds a good thing and obtains favor of the Lord."[56]

What we need to do as women is to seek and develop relationships with our heavenly Father and do His

---

[56] Proverbs 18:22

will, and all else will follow. Let God's will be done in our lives, and He (God) will give us the desires of our hearts. When we get in the way of God, we mess up every time; to see how this may be true, let's look back at our last few relationships, or look at the one we may be in now. As we look, let's recall the Scripture, "What therefore God hath joined together, let no man put asunder."[57]

I now understand better what Paul meant when he said, "I wish that all men were like I myself am [in this matter of self-control]. But each has his own special gift from God, one of this kind and one of another. But to the unmarried people and to the widows, I declare that it is (good, advantageous and wholesome) for them to remain [single] even as I do. But if they have no self-control (restraint of their passions), they should marry. For it is better to marry than to burn."[58] "Do you not know that your body is the temple (the very sanctuary) of the Holy Spirit

---

[57] Mark 10:6-9
[58] 1 Corinthians 7:7-9, Amplified

Who lives within you, whom you have received [as a Gift]
from God? "[59]

This is saying that we should honor God and bring
glory to Him in our bodies. Every time we commit
adultery, if we are married or fornicate, we are not only
sinning against, and disrespecting, our bodies, but, first and
foremost, we are sinning against God. Some women grow
up being abused or seeing their mothers being abused and
think that this is the way of life. Or, as children, they grow
up unloved by their fathers, so that, when they grow up,
they think the only way to get close to a man is to have sex;
or they think that having a baby will help keep a man.

I am here to tell you, that this is not the way. The
way for us to be free of all abuse is first to receive Jesus as
our Lord and Savior, get baptized, and start a relationship
with God—our own personal relationship. I remember my
mother telling me, "Why buy the cow, when the milk is

[59] 1 Corinthians 3:16-17, Amplified

free?" I know a lot of you have heard that one. Well, it's true. As women, we have to subject ourselves to God—to the powers that are ordained by God to give us the strength to maintain and keep our bodies as a living sacrifice—holy and acceptable unto God—which is your reasonable service. And, trust me, I know it's hard. "I know, when I would do good, evil is present with me. For I know that nothing good dwells within me, that is in my flesh, I can will what is right, but I cannot perform it. [I have the intention and urge to do what is right, but no power to carry it out]. For I fail to practice the good deeds I desire to do, but the evil deeds, that I do not desire to do it is no longer I doing it [it is not myself that acts], but the sin [principle], which dwells within me [fixed and operating in my soul]."[60]

This is why our blessings are in a holding pattern. It's not that God doesn't want us to receive our blessings;

---

[60] Romans 7:15-17

we are holding them back and stopping them by being disobedient to God's commandments. And we do this just because a guy is pressing us for sex—because we like him and we feel that if we don't give him any that he will go somewhere else. Let him go, I say. If that's all we are worth to him, it's not much. "For to be carnally minded is death; but to be spiritually minded is life and peace. Because the carnal mind is enmity against God: for it is not subject to the law of God, neither indeed can be. So then they that are in the flesh cannot please God."[61] And, "...if any man has not the Spirit of Christ, he is none of His."[62]

As believers, we must be continually cleansing, which allows us intimate fellowship with God. We have to remember that the flesh or sinful nature in us is a constant threat in our lives, and we must constantly and consistently put this sinful nature to death through the Holy Spirit who

---

[61] Romans 8:6-8
[62] Romans 8:9

dwells within us. We must admit our sins and seek

forgiveness and cleansing from God on a daily basis.

We don't have to resort to lowering ourselves to the

level of our fleshly and sinful nature, because our Father

owns everything, and He wants nothing but the best for His

daughters. Whatever we are seeking, we need to seek it

from the Most High God, mean it in our hearts, and He will

deliver us. I know that this is true, because He delivered me

from adultery and fornication—adultery during my

separation and fornication after my divorce.

The Separation

"If thou knowest the gift of God, and who it is that

saith to thee, Give me to drink; thou wouldest have asked of

him, and he would have given thee living water."[63]

---

[63] John 4:10

During my separation, I was desperately seeking counseling to save my marriage. As I mentioned before, in the midst of seeking, I went to a bishop whom I felt was straight (heterosexual) and asked him for help. In the midst of this help, we ended up sleeping together. Some help! After this happened, I knew it was wrong and, at this point, knew that this bishop couldn't help me.

I ended up meeting a woman who introduced me to another bishop who began counseling me. We became friends first, and then ended up dating. But I was still married; although, by this time, I had filed for a divorce. (Incidentally, when my husband found out that I had filed for a divorce—which he told me to do—then, all of a sudden, he wanted me back.) In any case, this second bishop and I also ended up fornicating, because, although I was still married on paper, in my heart, I was already divorced.

What was wrong with me? I was a hot mess and it wasn't funny. I was wrong—dead wrong—but, not intending to make excuses for my behavior, I feel it's important to share everything that happened to me. If it helps one other person in a similar situation to mine, it will have been worth it.

When I was married, my husband stopped having sex with me about two months into the marriage. I felt sick to my stomach and could not understand why he just stopped loving me after the short time we were married. I was on an emotional merry-go-round with this person and was losing everything—my business, my contracts, and my mind, just about. In hindsight, I now realize that he never loved me from the beginning. But God was with me, and I was covered by the blood of Jesus Christ.

Yes, I was wrong for committing adultery. I was so broken up from my marriage that I was looking for, and felt I was getting, what I needed from this man (the second counseling bishop) as though he was my husband. When I finally realized that he was not my husband and that he could not cover me, we split up and went our separate ways, because we could no longer act as though we were husband and wife. This is when I went back to my husband (because, as I mentioned previously, he had asked me back, although this turned out to be just another vicious plan on his part).

During my adulteress relationship, I prayed so hard to God. I had such serious repentance in my heart that I could hardly breathe. Feeling like the biblical woman who was caught in adultery, God took me to this scripture: "Jesus went unto the mount of Olives. And early in the morning he came again into the temple, and all the people came unto him; and he sat down, and taught them. And the scribes and Pharisees brought unto him a woman taken in adultery; and when they had set her in the midst, they say unto him, Master this woman was taken in adultery, in the very act. Now Moses in the law commanded us, that such should be stoned: but what sayest thou? (Meaning, what was Jesus' sentence for the woman?) This they said, tempting Him (Jesus) that they might have to accuse Him. But Jesus stooped down, and with His finger wrote on the ground, as though he heard them not. So when they continued asking Him, He lifted up himself and said unto them. He that is without sin among you let him first cast a stone at her. And again he stooped down, and wrote on the ground. And they which heard it, being convicted by their own conscience, went out one by one, beginning at the eldest, even unto the last: and Jesus was left alone, and the woman standing in the midst. When Jesus had lifted up himself, and saw none but the woman, He said unto her. Woman, where are those thine accusers? Hath no man condemned thee? She said, No man, Lord. And Jesus said unto her, neither do I condemn thee: go and sin no more."[64]

---

[64] John 8:1-10

Although this woman was not alone in the act—it takes two—and there was no mention of the guilty man (even though they obviously knew who he was, because they had caught them both in the act), at least God forgave her. He said to her, "Sin no more." Even though the man wasn't mentioned, I hope he, too, repented with a true repenting heart. God is no respecter of persons, and God knows who he was. Ultimately, nobody gets away with anything with God. He sees all, hears all, and knows all. Although the spirits that I was dealing with were some serious spirits—demonic spirits—God later told me all about myself, and He was with me; He never left me nor forsook me.

As women, we tend to look for love in all the wrong places, but now, since I have started seeking God for my every move, I am free. Thank you, Jesus! We must pray before we do anything and wait on the Lord for an answer, and when He gives us a sign, we must not ignore it.

"It's time to put the past behind us: and consider neither the things of old. Behold, God said He will do a new thing; now it shall spring forth; shall ye not know it? I will even make a way in the wilderness, and rivers in the desert."[65] We have to be in right standing with God to know when the new thing has come forth. The kingdom of God is at hand; the time for foolishness is gone. We are children of God; we are better than our fleshly and sinful nature, no matter what the devil says.

It's never too late to give our lives over to God as a living sacrifice—to live holy and acceptable to God. "Trust in the Lord with all thine heart: and lean not unto thine own understanding. In all thy ways acknowledge Him, and He shall direct thy paths."[66] "Better is the end of a thing than the beginning thereof: and the patient in spirit is better than

---

[65] Isaiah 43:18-19
[66] Proverbs 3:5-6

the proud in spirit."[67] "We can do all things through Christ

which strengtheneth us."[68]

Christian Holy Matrimony

"[A] house divided against itself shall not stand."[69]

Holy Matrimony means submitting ourselves one to

another in the fear of God. "Wives, submit yourselves unto

your own husbands, as it is fit in the Lord. Husbands, love

your wives and be not bitter against them."[70] "For the

husband is the head of the wife, even as Christ is the head

of the church: and he is the savior of the body."[71] "So ought

men to love their wives as their own bodies. He that loveth

his wife loveth himself."[72] "And whatsoever ye do, do it

heartily, as to the Lord, and not unto men: Knowing that of

---

[67] Ecclesiastes 7:8
[68] Philippians 4:13
[69] Matthew 12:25
[70] Colossians 3:18-19
[71] Ephesians 5:23
[72] Ephesians 5:28

the Lord ye shall receive the reward of the inheritance: for ye serve the Lord Christ. But he that doth wrong shall receive for the wrong, which he hath done: and there is no respect of persons."[73]

"Do not lie to one another, seeing that ye have put off the old man with his deeds: And have put on the new man, which is renewed in knowledge after the image of him that created him."[74] We must try to remember that "We are troubled on every side yet not distressed; we are perplexed, but not in despair. Persecuted, but not forsaken; cast down but not destroyed."[75] It is also good to remember that "For which cause we faint not; but though our outward man perish, yet the inward man is renewed day by day. For our light affliction, which is but for a moment, worketh for us a far more exceeding and eternal weight of glory. While we look not at the things which are seen, but at the things

[73] Colossians 3:23-25
[74] Colossians 3:9-10
[75] Corinthians 4:8-9

which are not seen: for the things which are seen are

temporal (temporary) but the things which are not seen are

eternal."[76]

No matter what it looks like, let us keep our faith

and trust in God with all our hearts. "Trust in the LORD

with all thine heart; and lean not unto thine own

understanding. In all thy ways acknowledge him, and he

shall direct thy paths."[77] If we are in an abusive

relationship, know that God is love; anything not done in

love is not of God, and no one has the right to abuse us. We

should never feel that we need to stay in an abusive

relationship. Abusive relationships are not healthy for us or

for our children, if we have them.

---

[76] Corinthians 4:16-17
[77] Proverbs 3:5-6

Marriage

"[A] house divided against itself shall not stand."[78]

The exclusive sexual relationship between a husband and a wife points to the exclusive commitment of total responsibility for each other. Spiritually, the act itself must be offered to God with intention and in thanksgiving, with both husband and wife acknowledging that God is the Author of their Love. Intercourse is pleasurable, not merely because there is sensual gratification, but because it expresses the joyful oneness of husband and wife. Each partner who offers sex to one another is a precious gift to the other—a gift exclusively preserved solely for that one man and one woman in holy matrimony.

The sexual union is sacramental in the sense that it's an outward sign and an inner commitment of love—a sacrament that is recognized as a gift from God. The union is more than physical, because from it emerges a spiritual

---

[78] Matthew 12:25

gift and knowledge that no man can separate. Such fulfillment is both the need and the right of the husband and wife alike. "For the wife does not have [exclusive] authority and control over her own body, but the husband [has his rights]; likewise also the husband does not have [exclusive] authority and control over his body, but the wife [has her rights]."[79]

In love for Christ is to be found the bond of oneness and the determination of the quality and strength of love for each other. Forgiving your mate whom you love is a creative force within marriage, deriving its nature from the experience of Christ's forgiving love. It will act as mercy, forgiving when there seems no adequate reason to forgive, and as grace, freely given with no promises demanded. It is creative love, suffering to achieve a high spiritual end. Marriage is endowed with spiritual significance when each partner is enabled by love to transcend his own self-

---

[79] Corinthians 7:4, Amplified

centeredness and identify himself with the well-being and concerns of his/her mate. Love is the sense that marriage is a divine order, which is binding between the two, which came from God witnessing, they became one. Paul comprehends marriage obligations for the husband under the principle of love, its highest standard being the love of Christ for His Church. (Col. 3:19; Eph. 5:25, 28) [80]

Sometimes, when we think we are in love with someone, we are actually in love with what we think the other person may be able to give us. This can be considered "conditional" love. Love, at its highest level, demands nothing in return. It's love for the sake of loving. Love is an inner quality that sees good—everywhere and in everyone. True love is given freely with no strings attached, unlike in my marriage. Love is real, it works, and it's gentle. I feel that love—true love—is the strongest tool we have to work

---

[80] The preceding paragraph is paraphrased from The Zondervan Pictorial Bible Dictionary, Zondervan Publishing House, 1967, p. 512.

with; it gives us patience to handle any and every situation

that we might come up against in our marriages.

MEN WHO WOULD RUIN A WOMAN'S LIFE

Low Down, Down Low

When one has been through any or all of what I have been through—whether with a boyfriend or a husband and whether we are talking about abuse, adultery, fornication, homosexuality, or whatever—and we then meet other men, with each new man, we can't help thinking to ourselves, "Is this man going to be like this, too?" And then we may find ourselves reflecting back on our previous relationship(s) and asking other questions, like why did this happen to me? And why did he *do* this to me? And why did he *lie*? And many other such questions.

Even though we may have God in our lives, there are still some unanswered questions. Perhaps you can't feel what I feel, not having been where I've been; perhaps these questions don't bother you. Or maybe you can feel me, but you can't feel it the way it happened to me. I suspect,

though, that if you are reading this book and have gotten

this far, you probably have some of these unanswered

questions in your life.

The most important question—not only for me, but

for anybody who has experienced abuse, cheating, adultery,

fornication, lies, and such—is: *Who has the right to ruin*

your life? Who has the right to live a double life—to live a

lie—while leaving a trail of destruction behind him? Is it

your husband, who claims to be a heterosexual, but every

now and then wants to sleep with other men and/or other

women? Is it your boyfriend who is always at his boy's

house playing Playstation 2, but when you confront him

about it when he gets home, he gets an attitude and storms

out? (I guess he just can't get enough of that NBA Live.)

I ask you, who? Who has the right? Do governors or

senators have the right because of their position? What

about a well-respected community leader or businessman,

perhaps a teacher, or the bishop over your church congregation? Who? I ask you. Who has the right?

What I love about God and his disciples in the biblical days is that His disciples knew Him. In Acts, Chapter 10, Verse 34, "Peter opened his mouth, and said, Of a truth I perceive that God is no respecter of persons." Even though Peter knew that God, his leader, was of the truth, Peter still strayed from the will of God. Looking at today's society, doesn't this sound familiar?

So I ask you, who has the right to ruin your life, without your permission? What makes it difficult to nip this kind of thing in the bud is that one never knows what is actually going on in another person's life, only what they share with us—only the face they show us, while hiding all the rest. These men who call themselves on the "down low" lie about who they are from the first time we meet them. Then we spend a decade (or more) of our lives with them, after which it seems as through our life has passed us by.

Again, I ask you, who has the right, against your wishes and against your hopes and dreams, to destroy those very hopes and dreams that you have envisioned since your childhood days?—the vision and dream of a union of one male and one female, joined together in holy matrimony, the two becoming one and going forth, being fruitful, and multiplying. Now we have a problem.

Who are these men who don't consider themselves gay, bisexual, or homosexual, but call themselves heterosexuals or "down low" and are sleeping with both men and women? Such "down low" men generally have no respect for their wives, girlfriends, or anyone else they decide to have unprotected sex with. These men don't care about their own protection, let alone anybody else's. They are spreading their HIV and STD's while jeopardizing women's lives.

"Down low" means a person who is living a lie and trying to cover up the truth while jeopardizing innocent women's lives. In my opinion, the name "down low" is too good for them. I call them "low down" because I have to keep it clean. But make no mistake, we are talking about men who are HIV carriers, STD carriers, and only care about themselves and their lust—like in Sodom and Gomorrah. We are talking about married men who are sleeping with other married as well as single men. We are talking about the carriers of demonically influential spirits that are killing our children and destroying our families.

The diseases these men carry do not discriminate. You can be black, white, Asian, or Hispanic; you can be a high school or college student with a promising life ahead of you; you can be rich or poor; you can be Christian, Buddhist, Islamic; you can be a well-known football star, an actor or actress, or a talk show host; you can be a baby, a child, a teenager, a mother or father, or a grandmother or grandfather; *it doesn't matter, because these diseases don't discriminate.*

Can we see what's happening to the human race? Believe it or not, we are all in this together, because it's our children, grandchildren, godchildren, friends, family members, and the next generation that will carry forth our community who are dying of this deadly disease (HIV, AIDS). And part of the reason that it's happening is that no one wants to talk about it. No one is taking it seriously enough; no one is taking *life* seriously enough.

In addition, too many women are keeping their relationship situations secret and are suffering in silence, because they are afraid to expose the demon(s) that are in their homes. Some of these women fail to speak out, because society tells us that we shouldn't bring men down. These are not men, though; let's not misrepresent "real men." These "down low" men put up a façade—false images made up to look like good and faithful men, when, in reality, they are unfaithful, promiscuous, and deviant liars, little better than animals. "Professing themselves to be

181

wise they became fools and changed the glory of the
uncorruptible God into an image made like to corruptible
man, and to birds, and fourfooted beasts, and creeping
things."[81]

These men do not take protective sex seriously, or,
more to the point, are not taking *our lives* seriously. We
only have one life to live on this earth. And even our
marriages are being destroyed by the men who now call
themselves "down low" men—the 21st century men of
Sodom and Gomorrah, one could say. God says, "My
people are destroyed for lack of knowledge: because thou
hast rejected knowledge, I will also reject thee, that thou
shalt be no priest to Me: seeing thou hast forgotten the law
of God, I will also forget thy children."[82] As we can see,
this whole thing ultimately turns into a curse.

---

[81] Romans 1:22-23
[82] Hosea 4:6

As women, we are not powerless in these situations—unless we let men take advantage of us because we are afraid of what we might lose by standing up for ourselves. What we might lose in such situations is far less than what we stand to gain by insisting on our rights, by turning away these demons, and by allowing the Lord God to guide us in our relationship choices. We have the power to take matters into our own hands. We have the power to educate ourselves and our children about the dangers of unprotected sex. We have the power to refuse sex to any man who refuses to be tested for HIV. And we have the power to demand protection where there is any doubt whatsoever. No test or no protection, then no sex—and that's final. And what's more, if a man refuses either, we have the power to ask ourselves and God whether such a man is actually right for us.

Characteristics of Men Who Would Ruin Your Life

"Take heed that no man deceive you."[83]

"For we ourselves also were sometimes foolish, disobedient, deceived, serving divers[e] lusts and pleasures, living in malice and envy, hateful, and hating one another. But after that the kindness and love of God our Savior toward man appeared. Not by works of righteousness which we have done, but according to his mercy he saved us, by the washing of regeneration, and renewing of the Holy Ghost."[84]

If we are honest with ourselves, we must admit that what we want is not always what we get, although maybe we do sometimes; it all depends on what we want. The important thing is being able to see ahead of time whether a thing or a person is really going to give us what we want. Or whether it or they will turn out to be exactly what we

---

[83] Matthew 24:4
[84] Titus 3:3-4

184

don't want. We must educate ourselves by understanding that there are recognizable characteristics of men who are out to destroy a women's life—men who put on a wholesome face while living an unwholesome life. (Note: we are talking only about these kind of men in this section of this chapter.)

As women, we tend to look for love in all the wrong places. Yes, we want to be loved, but let's keep this in perspective, and let's stop being complacent. We want to settle for less, instead of waiting for God's best; we get impatient instead of waiting, and we fail our test. A friend of mine once told me that I was a number one draft choice and that I was acting as a free agent—meaning that I should never have to settle for second best when it comes to relationships, and I have the power to choose who, when, and where when it comes to relationships. The truth hurts, but it will set us free. As women, we go around life wanting love, needing to be loved, and end up being in fake-love relationships, because, at the time, it feels right. We were given signs that it wasn't right, but either we weren't paying attention or we are simply ignoring the signs, and so we keep going back.

We even blame ourselves for not being able to hold on to a man. First of all, we must realize that a lot of men are not trying to hold on to us; it is a temporary thing for some men. Sex is all some want, and when you give it up, it's all over, because he has gotten what he wanted. I remember my mother saying, "Why buy the cow when the milk is free?" Let's remember that saying; I'm sure we have all heard it before. Personally, I'm finally coming to grips with that saying and seeing just how true it is.

Many men have told me that sex doesn't mean anything to them; if you've had one, you've had them all, they say. Are we hearing what is being said? If it's 'had one, had them all', then ask the man, 'Then why are you still trying to have sex with me?' Why are we still with such a man? We should be walking away—and fast! This is

a man who is disrespectful and who couldn't care less

about our self-worth or morals, because he doesn't have

any.

Other men are out there who are set on destroying a

strong woman's self esteem. Some do so simply because

they are not happy in their lives. Others do it because they

feel threatened by strong women. I have met many men

who have tried to kill my self-esteem, because I was sure

about who I was and what I wanted out of life. If we are,

say, a business owner or maybe have a high position in a

corporation, some men will treat us nice in order to reel us

in with their kindness. When we have taken the bait, then

they drop the bomb on us. They say, after a few months,

that they are not ready for a committed relationship. Or

they say that they don't know if we are the right one. Some

men will first tell us that they are not in any other

relationship, and they will wine and dine us and act as

though they want to be in a relationship with us. But, after a few months, they will say that they have changed their mind or that they have been seeing someone else but aren't sure about this person yet—as though expecting us to wait around until they can decide.

We need to wake up! This guy just did us a favor. He just told us exactly who and what he is. He is a man who is lying to get sex—a man who may even be lying about having someone else in his life (whom he might be interested in, but he'll let us know… sometime when it suits him) in order to string us along. We need to stop satisfying a man's needs in this way. If he is serious about us, he will do the right thing, and having casual sex is not the right thing.

If we listen carefully, we will see and hear the signs. If we listen closely to his conversation, we will soon find out where he is coming from. The Bible says, "Out of the abundance of the heart, the mouth speaketh."[85] In this way, we will gradually be able to stop getting caught up in love in the wrong places.

Then, we have the married men—married men who act publicly as though they are not married, or who act as though they are separated but still live under the same roof, sleeping in the basement, they tell people. Such men say, "Me and my wife have an understanding; we are still together until our son or daughter graduates from high school. We don't want to do this to the children." In truth, the only person who usually knows about this arrangement is the man who told you; the wife doesn't know anything about it. I personally know some men who have had false divorce papers made up just to get sex.

As women, we must understand that we are not alone; many have been fooled by the enemy. I say to you all, seek God for your comfort, for He will never leave you

---

[85] Matthew 12:34

or forsake you. We need to take a step back from our relationships—particularly if they seem so wonderful that we can hardly breathe. We need to let the smoke clear a little and try to gain a fuller understanding of what we are really dealing with. True self-worth is worth more than a temporary feel-good.

Love is important to a lot of women, but we have to be equally yoked. When we enter a relationship, the man should know what we want, and we should know what he wants. And, first and foremost, both man and woman should have a relationship with God. If we are not on the same page, nine times out of ten, things are not going to change. And there are men who will act as though they are on the same page just to get sex. We need to stop being so quick to give it up, because after we give it up, this kind of man is gone—on to the next woman who is vulnerable to his smooth talking, lying self.

We also need to stop thinking that by getting pregnant by a man it's going to make that man stay. This is a 'No, No, Momma's baby, Daddy's maybe.' Women who have been through this need to start mentoring young girls before they make mistakes that they will pay for maybe for years afterwards. We need to let them know that their self-worth is worth more than gold and that having a baby out of wedlock is a big mistake. Don't get me wrong, mistakes do happen; if they do, then we must pick up the pieces and then try not to make the same mistakes again.

We, as older women, need to stop the 'player hating' toward one another, the backstabbing, the envy, and the jealousy. We need to come together collectively with no other motive involved except to help build young girls' self-esteem and show them the road map for a solid foundation, because the devil is out to steal, kill, and destroy them every chance he gets.

Where are the family values that once mattered? Where are the "real men," as opposed to the "down low," "low down" men? The AIDS virus is real, and it's deadly; we are losing thousands to this disease in our high schools and colleges. Many children will not reach the age of eighteen due to drugs and gun violence; many will not even know what might have been ahead of them in their lives. More and more men and women, and boys and girls, are moving toward homosexual (gay and lesbian) relationships. Satan is real and is killing, stealing, and destroying many lives. Commitment is gone; family values are being destroyed. It hurts me to see that what was once important to the human race does not seem to matter anymore. People are out to get what they can get, at any cost and by any means necessary, no matter who it hurts or destroys, while we as Christians walk around as though we have blinders on our eyes. I truly believe we are at the end of our time and that God will return soon.

HOPE FOR A NEW DAY

Christ is Coming

The answer to all our prayers lies in the coming of Christ. In the meantime, we need to get ready for His coming. What good is wealth if we have no one to share it with? What good is any material thing if we are not ready for the coming of Christ? What good is it reaching fame and fortune if we are still going to hell? We need to start focusing on the coming of Christ more than on relationships, material goods, fame and fortune, and other such earthly things; what good is any of it if we loose our life in the end?

Words of Encouragement

We have the power to learn how to apply the word of God to our daily walk to overcome every attack of the devil. I would like to share with you in this next section some things that will help us protect ourselves and our families, help us speak life and not death into our lives, and show us that we can have power and authority over our lives, along with healing and prosperity.

When we turn our lives over to God, we become new people, all things in our lives become new, and our old selves are gone. We have to start using the power and authority that God has invested in us to kick the devil out. We are covered by the blood of Jesus, and His angels protect us. No matter what we come up against in our lives—no matter how seemingly terrible and/or painful— God has already prepared a way out for us.

In the midst of being challenged by the devil and his demons in our lives, we need to start becoming more aware of what we say and of how we speak. The following section offers some scriptures that we can use in our everyday walk—no matter whether we are at work and our boss gets to us, or we are in church and one of the saints gets to us (smile)! Whether the evil attacks come from a family member, a boyfriend, or a husband, we can use these scriptures as weapons to wage war against them and to make the devil flee—like Archangel Michael with his sword. This is not a fight against flesh and blood, but against the powers of darkness and the principalities of evil.

Scriptures for Protection

When we are 'attacked by the devil,' we can use the following scriptures for our protection and to help us remain aligned with God and His will for us.

"Let the weak say, I am strong."[86]

"In all these things we are more than conquerors through Him that loved us."[87]

---

[86] Joel 3:10
[87] Romans 8:37

"Death and life are in the power of the tongue: and they that love it shall eat the fruit thereof."[88] In other words, words kill, and words give life; they can be either poison or fruit—and it's up to us to choose.

"For by your words you will be justified and acquitted, and by your words you will be condemned and sentenced."[89] Out of the overflow of the heart, the mouth speaks. It's our heart, not the dictionary, that gives meaning to our words. A good person produces good deeds and words, season after season, whereas an evil person is blight on the orchard.

It's important to point out—for us to remember—that every careless word we use will eventually come back to haunt us; there will be a time of Reckoning. Words are powerful; take them seriously. Words can be our salvation, and words can also be our damnation. Certain people have

---

[88] Proverbs 18:21
[89] Matthew 12:37

no right to speak into our lives. We need to listen with the spirit to what people are speaking over us; and we need to stop always agreeing when we don't know what we are agreeing to.

"Submit yourselves, therefore to God. Resist the devil, and he will flee from you."[90] In other words, we need to let God work His will in us. We need to yell a loud "No!" to the Devil and then watch him scamper. We need to say a quiet "yes" to God, and he'll be there in no time. We need to quit dabbling in sin. To purify our inner lives. To quit playing the field, because, when we hit bottom, we cry our eyes out. The fun and games are over. We need to get serious—really serious. We need to get down on our knees before God; it's the only way we will get on our feet.

"When the Son sets you free, you will be free indeed"[91] What Jesus meant here is that anyone who

---

[90] James 4:7
[91] John 8:36

chooses a life of sin is trapped in a dead-end life and is, in fact, a slave. A slave is a transient, who can't come or go at will. The Son, though, has an established position and has the run of the house. So, if the Son sets you free, you are free, through and through.

"Lest Satan should get an advantage of us: for we are not ignorant of his devices."[92] This means, we must be aware of Satan's schemes so that he will not outwit us.

God has given us power and authority over our lives and the lives of our families. This is really something worth rejoicing over—something worth shouting about! Here's what the Bible says about power and authority—the power and authority that we, too, have.

"When the seventy-two returned with joy and said, 'Lord, even the demons submit to us in your name.' Jesus replied, 'I saw Satan fall like lightning from heaven. I have given you authority to trample on snakes and scorpions and

[92] 2 Corinthians 2:11

to overcome all the power of the enemy; nothing will harm you. However, do not rejoice that the spirits submit to you, but rejoice that your names are written in heaven.' At that time, Jesus, full of joy through the Holy Spirit, said, 'I praise you, Father, Lord of heaven and earth, because you have hidden these things from the wise and learned, and revealed them to little children. Yes, Father, for this was your good pleasure. All things have been committed to me by my Father. No one knows who the Son is except the Father, and no one knows who the Father is except the Son and those to whom the Son chooses to reveal him.' Then he turned to his disciples and said privately, 'Blessed are the eyes that see what you see. For I tell you that many prophets and kings wanted to see what you see but did not see it, and to hear what you hear but did not hear it."[93]

The prophets and kings didn't get so much as a whisper. In the same way, what I write and share in my

---

[93] Luke 10:17-23, NIV and The Message Parallel Bible

writings is not for everyone—only for those who need what I have to say at certain times in their lives. Not every thing we do is for everybody; we can't spread our pearls amongst swine. Of our dreams and visions, sometimes we have to be quiet until it's the right time to talk.

We have the power to break every stronghold over our minds, bodies, and souls in the name of Jesus. All we have to say is, "I command you to loose me in the name of Jesus. Come out of me right now in the name of Jesus!" We can call them out in the name of that stronghold.

As the Bible says, with the word of God, you will know the truth, and the truth will set you free.

Prosperity

"For you are becoming progressively acquainted with and recognizing more strongly and clearly the grace of our Lord Jesus Christ (His kindness, His gracious

generosity, His underserved favor and spiritual blessing),
[in] that though He was [so very] rich, yet for your sakes
He became [so very] poor, in order that by His poverty you
might become enriched (abundantly supplied)."[94]

We need to meditate day and night on the word of
God. We are trees, replanted in Eden, bearing fresh fruit
every month, never dropping a leaf, always in blossom.
Whatever we do prospers. We should be winning souls
everyday and encouraging people on a regular basis. We
are not defeated, but we are prospering and victorious. Our
mind, body, spirit, finances, marriage, relationships, past
and present, and everything in every area of our lives is
prosperous. "I have given and it shall be given unto me:
good measure, pressed down, and shaken together, and
running over, shall men give into my bosom. For with the
same measure that I mete it shall be measured to me."[95]

---

[94] 2 Corinthians 8:9, Amplified
[95] Luke 6:38

This is where we need to watch our words and how we treat people. Did we know that when we give, it is considered a fragrant offering, an acceptable sacrifice, pleasing to God, and that from that giving, God will meet all our needs according to His glorious riches in Christ Jesus?[96] When we help people in need, this is credited to our account with God. As Paul says in his Epistle to the Philippians, "Yet it was good of you to share in my troubles. Moreover, as you Philippians know, in the early days of your acquaintance with the gospel, when I set out from Macedonia, not one church shared with me in the matter of giving and receiving, except you only; for even when I was in Thessalonica, you sent me aid again and again when I was in need. Not that I am looking for a gift, but I am looking for what may be credited to your account. I have received full payment and even more: I am amply supplied, now that I have received from Epaphroditus the

---

[96] Philippians 4:18-20

gifts you sent. They are a fragrant offering, an acceptable sacrifice, pleasing to God. And my God will meet all your needs according to his glorious riches in Christ Jesus."[97]

Not everybody is going to help us in our times of need, and sometimes it will be those who call themselves friends who will not be there for us. On the other side of it, there are those who would try to be our friends—putting on the face of friendship—only for what they think they can get out of the deal.

I have had to become increasingly careful since I have been writing books. People have tried to befriend me just to get into my business—demon spirits who are only interested in getting the latest gossip back to the backbiters. Certain pastors have called only to get free books, saying they need them for this and that but couldn't find them in the book stores. They lied just to get free stuff, saying that they would send me some of their books in return. If I ever

---

[97] Philippians 4:14-19

received them, then you did, too (smile)! People whom I have never met in my life have called me or emailed me saying that they want to do interviews with me. Some of them really only wanted to get free press kits with books.

The devil is a liar, I say. I tried the spirit by the spirit; I knew all along who they were, because I'm connected to God through the Holy Spirit. When we start a business or write a book, we must not let people freeload off us. I don't see a lot of pastors working for free. The ones who try to freeload are the main ones quoting the scripture, "For the workman is worthy of his meat."[98] It's true; everyone should get paid for his or her work. If there are some things that we are to give away free, we just need to know who we should give them away to. The books I write cost money to publish. I don't have a publisher running to give me an advance. My books are put together with a lot of hard work and a lot of hard-earned money. No

---

[98] Matthew 10:9

one did anything for me for free. So when some people seem to always have their hands extended for something free, we need to flee!

I shared the preceding as an illustration of how people want and expect something for nothing. But this is not how our prosperity comes. When someone sows into a ministry, whether it's a church ministry, book ministry, music ministry, or whatever, their account is credited by God. We just read this in the Bible. This is how our prosperity comes. "For with what judgment ye judge, ye shall be judged: and with what measure ye mete, it shall be measured to you again."[99]

How can we expect to prosper if we are not doing it by what the scriptures say? In Malachi, God says, "I will open you the window of heaven, and pour you out a blessing, that there shall not be room enough to receive it." And He goes on to say, "And all nations shall call you

---

[99] Matthew 7:2

blessed.[100]" When we confess with our mouths to walk in the favor of God on our jobs, in our business deals, in our schools, and with other people, God's favor will rest upon us. God says, "He bless the righteous and surround them with His favor as with a shield."[101] We should be speaking favor and success on our lives right now in the name of Jesus and asking that He will increase our wisdom, knowledge, understanding, discernment, stature, and our favor with God and man. We can do all things through Christ Jesus who strengthens us. All things are possible to him that believes. The choice is ours.

Healing

"Surely he took up our infirmities and carried our sorrows, yet we considered him stricken by God, smitten by him, and afflicted. But he was pierced for our iniquities;

---

[100] Malachi 3:10-12
[101] Psalms 5:12

the punishment that brought us peace was upon him, and by his wounds we are healed. It was our pains he carried—our disfigurements, all the things wrong with us. It was our sins that did that to him, that ripped and tore and crushed him— our sins! He took the punishment, and that made us whole. Through his bruises, we get healed. We've all been like sheep who've wandered off and gotten lost. We've all done our own thing, gone our own way, and God has piled all our sins, everything we've done wrong on him.[102] 'Jesus personally bore our sins in His [own] body on the tree [as on an altar and offered Himself on it], that we might die (cease to exist) to sin and live to righteousness. By His wounds we have been healed.'[103] Christ redeemed us from the curse by becoming a curse for us, for it is written: 'Cursed is everyone who is hung on a tree. He redeemed us in order that the blessing given to Abraham might come to

---

[102] Isaish 53:4-12
[103] 1 Peter 2:24

the Gentiles (us) through Christ Jesus, so that by faith we might receive the promise of the Spirit.'"[104]

So, as we can see, we can use the power and authority that God has invested in us for us, our family, and our friends—for healing, for overcoming the attacks of the devil, and for praying for marriages, relationships, friendships, leaders, prosperity, and our children. All things are possible to him/her that believes.

"The eyes of the Lord range throughout the earth to strengthen those whose hearts are fully committed to Him."[105] So, let's get committed. "Praise the Lord, O my soul, and forget not all his benefits—who forgives all your sins and heals all your diseases, who redeems your life from the pit and crowns you with love and compassion, who satisfies your desires with good things so that your

---

[104] Galatians 3:13-14
[105] 2 Chronicles 16:9

youth is renewed like the eagle's."[106] "God is the same,

yesterday, today, and for ever."[107] In other words, He never

changes.

God wants the best for all His children. He says,

"Beloved, I pray that you may prosper in every way and

[that your body] may keep well, even as [I know] your soul

keeps well and prospers."[108] What I love about God is that

His words never return to Him void. He says, "So shall My

word be that goes forth out of My mouth: it shall not return

to Me void [without producing and effect, useless], but it

shall accomplish that which I please and purpose, and it

shall prosper in the thing for which I sent it. For you shall

go out [from the spiritual exile caused by sin and evil into

the homeland] with joy and be led forth [by your Leader,

the Lord Himself, and His word] with peace; the mountains

---

[106] Psalm 103:1-22
[107] Hebrews 13:8
[108] 3 John 2

and the hills shall break forth before you into singing, and all the trees of the field shall clap their hands."[109]

Somebody should be on the floor right about now, praising the Lord! Look at all the power He is trusting us with! Good God Almighty!

And what I'm telling you—it's all in the tongue. We speak bad things on our life all the time. Let's STOP, right now! Let's start right now changing the way we speak. Let's speak positively. When we want something, all we have to do is speak it, have faith, and believe that it is. Jesus says, "Have faith in God. I tell you the truth, if anyone says to this mountain, 'Go, throw yourself into the sea,' and does not doubt in his heart but believes that what he says will happen, it will be done for him. Therefore I tell you, whatever you ask for in prayer, believe that you have received it, and it will be yours. And when you stand praying, if you hold any thing against anyone, forgive him,

---

[109] Isaiah 55:11-12

so that your Father in heaven may forgive you your

sins."[110]

Here are the key points... first, in whatever we may

ask for, we need to have faith, believe, and have no doubt.

Second, we need to forgive everyone—anyone we may be

holding something against, whether it be grudges,

resentment, blame, or something else—as this will

definitely stop our blessings. It doesn't matter what they

have done to us; let's repent and forgive. This is the power

of faith. Once we get these basics down, we are on our

way. "He sent his word, and healed them, and delivered

them from their destructions."[111] Let's affirm, again and

again: I am healed! I am healed! I am healed!

---

[110] Mark 11; 22-26
[111] Psalms 107:20

Change Your Life

I offer you a prayer—for you and your life—in the matchless name of Jesus Christ:

"I Pray that the God of our Lord Jesus Christ, the glorious Father, may give you the Spirit of wisdom, knowledge, understanding, discernment, and revelation, so that you may know Him better, and that knowing Him personally, your eyes will be focused and clearer, so that you can see exactly what it is He is calling you to do. I pray also that the eyes of your heart may be enlightened in order that you may know the hope to which He has called you, the riches of His glorious inheritance in the saints, and His incomparably great power for us who believe. That power is like the working of His mighty strength, which He exerted in Christ when He raised Him from the dead and seated Him at His right hand in the heavenly realms, far above all rule and authority, power and dominion, and every title that can be given, from the galaxies to governments, no name and no power exempt from His rule, not only in the present age but also in the one to come. At the center of all of this, Christ rules the church. The church, you see, is not peripheral to the world; the world is peripheral to the church. The church is Christ's body, and God place all things under His feet and appointed Him to head over everything for the church, which is His body, the fullness of Him who fills everything in every way, in which Christ speaks and acts, by which He fills everything with His presence."[112]

A Prayer for Strength through the Spirit

"For this cause I bow my knees unto the Father of our Lord Jesus Christ, Of whom the whole family in heaven and earth is named, That he would grant you, according to the riches of his glory, to be strengthened with might by his Spirit in the inner man; that Christ may dwell

---

[112] Ephesians 1:17-23

in your hearts by faith; that ye, being rooted and grounded in love, May be able to comprehend with all saints what is the breadth, and length, and depth, and height; And to know the love of Christ, which passeth knowledge, that ye might be filled with all the fullness of God. Now unto him that is able to do exceeding abundantly above all that we ask or think, according to the power that worketh in us, Unto him be glory in the church by Christ Jesus throughout all ages, world without end. Amen."[113]

If we are serious about living this new resurrection life with Christ, let's act like it. Let's not shuffle along, eyes to the ground, absorbed with the things right in front of us. Let's look up and be alert to what is going on around Christ. That's where the action is. Let's see things from His perspective. Let's declare our old lives dead. Our new lives, which are our real lives—even though invisible to spectators—are with Christ in God. He is our life. When

---

[113] Ephesians 3:14-21

214

Christ (who is our real life, remember) shows up again on this earth, we will show up, too—the real you and me, the glorious you and me.

Meanwhile, let's be content with obscurity, like Christ. And that means killing off everything connected with the ways of death: sexual promiscuity, impurity, lust, doing whatever we feel like whenever we feel like it, and grabbing whatever attracts our fancy. These things constitute a life shaped by things and feelings instead of by God. It's because of these kinds of things that God is about to explode in anger.

It wasn't that long ago that we were doing all these things and not knowing any better. But we know better now, so we need to make sure that it's all gone for good— bad temper, irritability, meanness, profanity, dirty talk, and so forth. Let's stop lying to one another. We're done with that old life. It's like a filthy set of ill-fitting clothes that we have stripped off and put in the fire. Now, we're dressed in a new wardrobe. Every item of our new way of life is custom-made by the Creator, with his label on it. All the old fashions are now obsolete. So, chosen by God for this new life of love, let's dress in the wardrobe God has picked out for us: compassion, kindness, humility, quiet strength, discipline, and so forth. Let's be even-tempered, content with second place, and quick to forgive an offence. Let's forgive as quickly and completely as God forgave us. And regardless of what else we put on, let's wear love. It's our basic, all-purpose garment. Let's never be without it.

We have to walk in love, so we can walk in victory, so people will see who we are in God.

A Fight to the Finish

Let's make no mistake… we are at war. Do we stand by and watch terrorists attack our country, destroy what we have worked for, and kill our families, friends, children, and fellow countryman? No, we fight back, and rightly so. In the same way, we need to fight against all the schemes of the devil and his evil spirits, wherever we may encounter them. We have the power. We have the choice. And we have the responsibility.

In the words of Paul the Apostle, "Finally, be strong in the Lord and in his mighty power. Put on the full armor of God so that you can take your stand against the devil's schemes. For our struggles is not against flesh and blood, but against the rulers, against the authorities, against the rulers, against the authorities, against the powers of this dark world and against the spiritual forces of evil in the heavenly realms. Therefore put on the full armor of God, so that when the day of evil comes, you may be able to stand your ground, and after you have done everything, to stand. Stand firm then, with the belt of truth buckled around your waist, with the breastplate of righteousness in place, and with your feet fitted with the readiness that comes from the gospel of peace.

"In addition to all this, take up the shield of faith, with which you can extinguish all the flaming arrows of evil one. Take the helmet of salvation and the sword of the Spirit, which is the word of God. And pray in the Spirit on all occasions with all kinds of prayers and requests. With this in mind, be alert and always keep on praying for all the saints.

"Pray also for me, that whenever I open my mouth, words may be given me so that I will fearlessly make known the mystery of the gospel, for which I am an ambassador in chains. Pray that I may declare it fearlessly, as I should."[114]

Amen!

---

[114] Ephesians 6:10-17

Notes

Printed in the United States
27830LVS00005B/121-138

9 780974 511221